ALEXANDER ELIOT's distinguished career includes having been a Guggenheim Fellow, a Japan Foundation Senior Fellow, and Art Director of *Time* magazine. A world traveler and lecturer, he lives in Venice, California.

Alexander Eliot's Mythology Series

The Universal Myths
The Global Myths
The Timeless Myths

THE
TIMELESS
MYTHS

*How Ancient Legends
Influence the Modern
World*

ALEXANDER ELIOT

TRUMAN TALLEY BOOKS/MERIDIAN

TRUMAN TALLEY BOOKS/MERIDIAN
Published by the Penguin Group
Penguin Books USA Inc., 375 Hudson Street, New York, New York 10014, U.S.A.
Penguin Books Ltd, 27 Wrights Lane, London W8 5TZ, England
Penguin Books Australia Ltd, Ringwood, Victoria, Australia
Penguin Books Canada Ltd, 10 Alcorn Avenue, Toronto, Ontario, Canada M4V 3B2
Penguin Books (N.Z.) Ltd, 182-190 Wairau Road, Auckland 10, New Zealand

Penguin Books Ltd, Registered Offices: Harmondsworth, Middlesex, England

Published by Truman Talley Books/Meridian, an imprint of Dutton Signet,
a division of Penguin Books USA Inc. First published in a hardcover edition by
The Continuum Publishing Company.

First Truman Talley Books/Meridian Printing, June 1997
10 9 8 7 6 5 4 3 2 1

 REGISTERED TRADEMARK——MARCA REGISTRADA

ISBN: 0-452-01126-4
CIP data is available.

Printed in the United States of America

For Jane Winslow Eliot,
who guards my lips
and guides my heart

Contents

Part 2: The Power of Images

Part 3: The Pursuit of Virtue

Preface

BY ROBERT A. F. THURMAN
Jey Tsong Khapa Professor
of Indo-Tibetan Studies
Columbia University

I am happy to write a word to open the door for the reader to enter Alex Eliot's mythosphere. This is his original and intriguing concept of a globe that permeates and envelops our habitual globes of fire, earth, water, and air. It is a globe of mindstuff that swirls with patterns and energies, coruscating with powers of individuals and groups, symbols and stories. This mythosphere is not less important because more intangible. It is more primary; it structures and controls the swirlings of gravity, magnetism, electricity, light, and heat. It is the collective mindfield of conscious beings, including microbes, bugs, dragons, fairies, elves, goblins, ghosts, angels, demons, gods, and even Gods, along with us eternally would-be humans.

In ancient India, Shakyamuni the Buddha was asked by an enthusiastic group of idealistic youths, "How does the enlightening heroine or hero perfect

and beautify the real universe as you see it, the buddhaverse?" This is the timeless messianic question;
"If we vow to save all living from suffering, what
makes success a realistic possibility, not merely a
sentimental urge?" Shakyamuni answers, "Noble
youths, a buddhaverse *is* a world of sentient beings—it springs from the aims of sentient beings!"
The Buddha anticipates Alex here, seeing the world
not primarily as a theater of solid objects, rocks
and seas and trees and suns and rays and star-
systems, but rather as an intersubjective mindfield
of conscious beings, from the tiniest microbes to
great, transuniversal Gods. The furniture, the real
estate, the hardware—it all gets structure from the
intersection of this infinity of consciousness. That
being so, it is possible for a bodhisattva heroine or
hero to transform a local universe of beings from a
mutual imprisonment in pain into a mutual exalta-
tion in delight, when she or he persuades all these
beings of the preferability of the more delightful
stories.

Exploring the mythosphere to find the more delightful story, this is the work of the mythospheric
aviators, the "mythonauts," among whom Alex
Eliot stands out today as a shining example. The
"more delightful" is of course not always the more
namby-pamby; it sometimes is the more grotesque,
scary, repulsive, realistic, unsettling, worrisome.
But in the depth of whichever of the eight or nine
main aesthetic "tastes," tragic, comic, horrific, heroic, miraculous, and so on, as discerned by the
classical Indians, those most sophisticated of literary critics, one finds a "bedmyth," a rock of truth,
illumination, transcendence, reconciliation, integra-

tion; whatever we call it, it is always the more enduringly delightful.

Alex the Mythonaut is a veteran voyager, adventurer of the mythstreams roaring round the sphere. He is a connoisseur of the various tastes of myths, utterly pluralistic, as at home with the great Lo Kuo of the Indochinese mythland as with the druidic gods of Eire or the great Egyptian, Biblical, and Olympian figures that most of us would find more familiar. Taking Nietzsche's hint, he selects for us many colorful strands and patches of mythic fabric and weaves for his fellow moderns, who stand shivering, "stripped of myth," homeless in the deepest sense, possible new clothes of meaning to comfort, protect, and energize. He does not pretend to make one uniform garment we all should wear; he is no dreary industrialist of myth. He is clearly grounded in the Greco-Euro-sphere, but his many shuttlings to the multiple moons of myth have made him familiar with and appreciative of the treasures of the entire sphere. So he performs a most valuable service, showing us the range of mythic magic around the sphere.

Not content with the timeless past, he shows how it permeates the uttermost contemporary, sharing his sojourns in museums and artist's lairs, illustrating the ongoing power of images revealed to us in Gauguin, Whistler, Picasso, Hopper, Pollock, de Kooning, and many other poets and painters. He is playful and wide-ranging: I was speechlessly enchanted at the prospect of the five *Demoiselles d' Avignon* from the mythospheric perspective: emergent from the birth of Zeus on Crete, interreflective with the Cretan el Greco's *Opening of the Fifth Seal*

and indeed The Book of Revelation itself, opening
a floodgate for African mythenergy in a powerful
recovery of an interconnected Europe, a special
baby's life saved by a puff of cigar-smoke! You'll
have to find the rest yourself.

Finally, mythonauts do not merely entertain,
they enterlight, they enterform, they move our
minds and hearts. Alex does not lead off our rocky,
watery globe into an escapist timelessness. His selected myths are timeless in that they all circle at the
event horizon of eternity, the brink of the always
unreachable because never abandoned absolute, the
solid conscious grace of infinity that is nothing to
us because it is just us and our everything as we
playfully enjoy and beautify dualities. He works at
the end with the pursuit of virtue, lightly inspiring
with joyful meanings, launching great purpose and
potential into the teeth of death and chaos—always
playful, humorous, gentle yet sincere.

This book is not to devour: savor it, live with
more quality, more heart, more soul—be a
mythonaut!

A Letter

Written to the Author to Be Read by the Reader

BY ELIOT DEUTSCH
Professor of Philosophy
and Chair of Graduate Studies
The University of Hawaii, Manoa

Dear Alex:

I am deeply honored to have been invited to prepare this foreword to your wonderful book *The Timeless Myths*—but may I do so in espitolary, rather than in the standard, rather dry, academic form? In this way I know I will be speaking more directly to you than to your readers who will be eavesdropping, as it were, on our conversation. Nevertheless, "forewording" your book in this manner will, I think, be more in keeping with that most bearable lightness of being which you so nicely exhibit in your work.

Aristotle, as you know, allowed that philosophy begins in wonder. Unfortunately, he failed to realize that it ought to end, as it were, with an even greater wonder—the kind that pervades *The Time-less Myths.* You speak about a "mythosphere" where "thinking, dreaming and imagining go on and on without even starting to cram our craniums. Mental furniture flies freely in and out, like breathing. Why? Because one's intellectual doors and windows stand wide open to an infinitely greater area." You go on to say that "we can't leap out of nature, nor do we exit the mythosphere. . . . Every man, woman and child on earth has a soul-right to the mythosphere's sun-warm orchard and her attic trunks crowded with curious delights. We're not exploiters, outsiders, students, or tourists either, in the mythosphere. We're home."

And so we have a new and quite marvelous myth—the mythosphere—which contains all manner of holy legends, creation stories, folktales and fairytales, sacred and not so sacred images of art and ritual artifacts. With your typical generosity of spirit you have included so much more in this sphere—and indeed why not?—than is typically the case with thinkers like Eliade and Ricoeur who believe that "myth narrates a sacred history, telling of events that took place in primordial time, the fabulous time of the 'beginnings.'" Yes, of course, there are creation myths and others that narrate 'beginnings'; but yes, there are also all manner of thoughts, dreams and images where, as you say, we "stand wide open to an infinitely greater area." You are, I think, very much on the right track. You tell us about Biblical and old Irish, Egyptian and Chinese, Greek and Indian myths and those of Plato, Goethe and a host of others.

At first I was somewhat puzzled by your inclusion of visual artworks in your mythosphere, for example, Picasso's "Demoiselles d'Avignon," "Whistler's Mother" and Breughel's "Massacre of the Innocents," which you describe so beautifully, and your recording of conversations you had with artists such as Edward Hopper. But then you write:

> Tearless nostalgia, the ache of loneliness, and finally the sense of romance just beyond reach, inform Hopper's creative work. Each of his canvases . . . tells a wordless story, but they're not illustrations of anything.

And then you consider his well-known *Nighthawks* where

> we're put near a city corner, at a midnight hour, looking across the street and in through the plate glass window of a bright-lit fast-food joint.

And you remark:

> Looking at *Nighthawks,* I sense an invisible fifth participant who hovers on our side of the street. A passerby like us, he observes the action from the dark, and in through the plate glass, with appreciative and yet rather terrible detachment. Darkly shimmering, mercurial and soon gone again is the artist's self, the actual nighthawk.

And then to me it all makes sense, for there is something revelatory in Hopper's work that, like all fine works of art, speaks entirely in its own visual terms.

Robert Graves, whom you no doubt have met at some point in your travels, has written that "mythology is the study of whatever religious or heroic legends are so foreign to a student's experience that he cannot believe them to be true." So let us ask: What does it mean to believe that a legend, or indeed an artwork, is true? Does mythology or art have anything at all to do with "truth" (understood in the common way as some kind of correspondence between statement and state of affairs)?

Hans-Georg Gadamer has convincingly shown to many of us how a sharp distinction, going back to the Greeks, has been drawn philosophically between *mythos* and *logos,* with the latter seen unhappily as an evolutionary advance over the former. *Logos*—truth-seeking and truth-telling—replaces, so it is believed, the fanciful, superstition-based tales that wrongly claim historical legitimacy. The *mythos/logos* dichotomy has always held that the two really deal with the same thing, namely offering *explanations* of the world (its origin, etc.) and of human experience, with the one clearly superior to the other. *Mythos* is fine for children and for "primitive" people; we, mature modern adults, have other and more important (scientific and rational) matters to attend to.

The great advantage, it seems to me, of your conception of an inclusive mythosphere is that we can simply set aside this *mythos/logos* business in favor of an understanding that myths, like art works, do not compete, as it were, with one another with regard to truth claims; instead they *present* rather than *represent* their content and thus have a special integrity of their own. Your mythosphere rightly contains various forms of symbolic discourse in which new forms of meaning are created and expressed. A myth, can we not all agree, like any work of art, has its own intentionality to present meaning precisely as the vivid, narrative form it is.

Myths, then, I'm sure *you*, at any rate, would agree, are neither true nor false; they are adequate or inadequate; they are alive or dead, which is to say that, while being as you remark "timeless," they either have or lack the power to evoke a meaningful response.

Your book, with its wise comments on the contemporary cultural and political scene and accounts of your personal experiences going back to childhood (your playing Hercules in the school play and accidentally knocking down the stage set) intermingled with the telling of innumerable tales, is I dare say unique and certainly should evoke a strong response in any sensitive reader. Your robust common sense, insatiable curiosity, playfulness and humor, all shine forth. There is much joy here and also an acknowledgment of terror and pain; and yes, even magic in your evocation of what resides and may be seen to reside in the mythosphere.

Here is a little fantasy (not to be confounded with the mythic) of my own. Together with other friends and families (for there should be young children about), we are sitting around a campfire late at night somewhere far away from any "information superhighway" (quite a tale going on there!) with spirits in hand and listening hour after hour to you telling (or better chanting in your richly resonant voice) sacred stories and all the rest and whatever new creations you might spontaneously bring forth. The star-bright sky, rather than distant, is near to us and we all feel cozy, at home, filled nevertheless with wonder.

Well, the next best thing for anyone is to read *The Timeless Myths,* preferably near a fireplace with the appropriate spirits very much in hand.

> With great respect and affection.
> Manoa, August 1995

The Importance
of Place

How do timeless myths keep spinning back into the mainstream of time, into history and personal experience? This happens thanks to religious ritual, folktale, fairytale, literature, painting, sculpture, architecture, music, dance, and so on. It also happens thanks to certain commandments, or moral and social injunctions, that have their roots in sacred legend. But that's not all. The constellations of stars in the sky remind us of many a myth; so do particular landscapes and sacred sites. One could write volumes on this theme without beginning to exhaust its possibilities. I'll enter the subject via Africa. From there I'll draw an Ariadne-thread through the Middle East, Australia, Italy, Ireland, and the rest of the world.

Africa

Yoruba storytellers of Nigeria begin each tale with the following full-blown phrase-chain: "Once upon a time, a time passes, a time is coming, a time will never finish upon the earth." Here's one of their stories concerning Tortoise, the Socrates of African lore.

"I'll collect all the wisdom of the world," Tortoise told himself. I'll stuff the whole lot into a great big gourd, which I'll hang at the top of the tallest tree. Then everyone will admire me."

The trouble was, when he tried to climb the tallest tree with the compendious gourd tied to his belly, the gourd got in the way. The sturdy Tortoise kept slipping down between the branches and falling with a dreadful thump to the ground. He'd land hard on his back, with the gourd on top of him. Yet he kept on trying and trying, for tortoises are creatures of slow, steady intensity.

Finally a snail took pity on him. "I'm little and foolish," the snail began, "but I can tell you one thing. If you swung that gourd over your shoulder and carried it up the tree on your back, the way I carry my shell, you'd find the going easier."

Tortoise thought that over. Then he said: "Plainly, all the wisdom of the world is not inside my gourd!" And he abandoned the whole project.

There are many ways to climb a tree, and many paths through the forest, the Twi people say. Yet in the Before Time only one path existed. On that single path, Grandfather Sky gave his daughter the name "Mpensaaduasa." The path overheard and later it repeated the name in Spider's ear.

When a spider weaves a web, does he follow many paths, or one? Many are the strands, naturally, yet they all stem from his own belly.

Grandfather Sky promised his daughter in marriage to anyone who could guess her name. He was hoping to acquire a brilliant son-in-law, but things did not work out as expected. Spider "guessed" the name, of course, and got the girl.

As for the indiscreet path, Grandfather Sky was so angry he beat it to pieces. That's why there are so many paths, besides the beaten one, today.

The Ga people of Ghana tell of three magicians who were traveling together and came to the bank of a rushing stream. There was no bridge, nor was there a boat. So the first magician spun a fine thread which he cast with an arching motion over the stream. Stepping lightly onto the thread, barely wetting his sandals in the process, he tiptoed to the other side.

The second magician didn't quite trust the thread. Instead, he dipped a crystal flask into the stream. Lo and behold, the entire river rushed into that little bottle and stayed. Having walked across on dry land, the second magician turned around and emptied out his flask, whereupon the river ran as merrily as before.

Left alone on the near side, the third magician stood fuming. From each of his fingers, scorching fire flamed. A stretch of the stream evaporated in the heat. Striding through the momentary opening, he rejoined his companions.

Which of the three was the greatest magician? Ga storytellers conclude with this unanswerable question.

Which magician do you like? The first crossed over creatively, by means of imagination. The second used the crystal flask of intellect, which takes things in—and lets them go again. The third flamed with willpower, concentration, and emotional force. We're talking about three different sorts of magic. The first belongs to dreamers and artists. The second belongs to professors and priests. The third belongs to performers and warriors.

One might equate the three magicians of the story with such classical figures as Homer, Pythagoras, and Alexander the Great. Among our twentieth-century equivalents would be Picasso, Einstein, and the passive-resistance warrior Mahatma Ghandi.

The Sefwi people offer a comparable tale which concerns three lovers. Its Arabian Nights, perfume persuades me that this one filtered down into Ghana from Moorish Africa:

Once in the kingdom of flowers there lived a beautiful young princess. Her skin was the color of dark honey, the tips of her toes and fingers gleamed like opals, her eyes were as bright as a lagoon at high noon, and her hair was as blue-black as midnight beneath a magnolia tree. Three young men courted her. The first possessed a magic mirror which enabled him to see things from far away. The second possessed a magic cord by means of which he could travel great distances in the wink of an eye. The third possessed a horsehair fly-whisk with the power of conferring life.

The princess was still too young to get married. The attentions of the three young men wearied her and also annoyed her father the king. As a result, all three were banished to a far country.

One day the first suitor looked in his magic mirror and discovered the princess lying dead atop a funeral pyre! The second suitor looped his magic cord around him and his companions. Instantly, the three found themselves back home at the funeral site. Reverently, the third suitor brandished his fly-whisk about the corpse. Nothing happened. With a deep sigh, the third suitor reverently laid the fly-whisk between her budding breasts and turned away.

She breathed again. She raised her arms, passed her hands across her face, and sat up smiling!

Who was the greatest lover? The man with the mirror, the man with the cord, or the man with the fly-whisk? Like the previous riddle of the three magicians, this one too is meant to be rhetorical. "Whether it be sweet or not sweet," the Sefwi storyteller concludes, "take a bit of it and keep the rest under your pillow."

To my mind the magic implements mentioned in this story refer to the reflective, ecstatic, and life-giving powers of art. But I believe the greatest lover was the princess herself: the half-formed soul awakening to life.

Ephesus and Jerusalem

What is the way to wisdom? The pre-Socratic philosophers associated with Ionian Greece recognized three broad pathways as winding in that general direction, namely History, Polymathy, and Reverie. The first way called for traveling and questioning, like Herodotus. The second way called for studying, testing, and trying, like Pythagoras. The third way was the most difficult. The inward path of *enantiodromia* meant riding a reversed intellectual current down, down into the depths of one's own experience.

"I searched myself!" Heraclitus proclaimed. "Although you travel every road, never shall you reach the soul's limits, for it has too deep a Word."

Heraclitus was careful to define "Word," or *Logos* as being "that which steers all things from within." Was he refering to the natural order of things, the harmony made manifest in weights, measures, and velocities? John the Evangelist, who had certainly read Heraclitus, expressed a different view in his gospel: "In the beginning was the Word, and the Word was with God, and the Word was God."

Johannes Kepler, who first enunciated the laws of planetary motion early in the seventeenth century, and whose system of infinitesmals laid the foundations for calculus, embraced both aspects of *Logos*. "Is it possible," he wrote, "that I can find god, whom I almost grasp with my fingers when I gaze into the universe of stars, within myself?"

Now if History, Polymathy, and Reverie, all tend toward wisdom, why not pursue all three?

I was driving through fragrant, spacious, mountain-cradled countryside in a land carpeted with wildflowers. Around me lay the tumbled relics of history-braided myth. My first stop was at a roadside marker, which read, in Turkish, French, and English: "The Cave of the Seven Sleepers." I followed a winding uphill path overgrown with poppies—the flowers from which come opium, hashish, and morphine. In ancient times, poppies were sacred to Morpheus, the god of sleep. Fifteen minutes of walking brought me to a cliff pierced with a number of narrow caverns carved from the living rock. Deserted now, the caves had once comprised a monastic retreat. Legend relates that "the Seven Sleepers" were early Christian fathers, condemned to death for refusing to worship the Roman Emperor Domitian as a god. Secretly assembled in the deepest of these caverns, they slept for centuries undisturbed. When at last Rome fell, the Seven Sleepers emerged, rubbing their starry eyes, to worship Christ in the waking state.

My second stop was at the archeological site of ancient Ephesus. In Greek and Roman times this became an immensely rich trade center where shopping was a way of life, artists and craftsmen prospered, aqueducts converged, and monuments fountained from the dry ground. The city center has been sweepingly excavated to present a wide blaze of marble ruins crisscrossed with memories of legendary men and women. The sculptors Polyclitus and Phidias, the philosophers Heraclitus and Simplicius, Alexander the Great, the lyricist Calimachus, Marc Antony, and Cleopatra walked here. So did John the Beloved Disciple, John the Evangelist, and John of Patmos—all of whom may, or may not, have been the same person.

From A.D. 49 to 52 Saint Paul made Ephesus his headquarters. Here he wrote letters to the Corinthians and the Colossians urging suppression of sexual passion and advocating the benign subjection of women. At Ephesus, Zeus himself was eclipsed by the goddess Artemis. and here the Amazon warrior-women of classical myth were revered as ancestral spirits. Hence the saint's well-meaning mysogeny rubbed Ephesians the wrong way. So did his drumbeat condemnation of "idolatry." Finally a silversmith named Demetrios, who specialized in precious reliquaries and statuettes, instigated a riot which forced Paul to flee the city.

My third stop was at the site of the vanished "Artemesion" or Temple of Artemis. It's now a stagnant pond whose waters are glimmeringly floored with slimy stone remains and topped by a single "restored" column. That solitary object with its wavering reflection resembled an admonitory finger thrusting upward from a watery blue-green first. Just who was being admonished? Myself, of course, to look and imagine. Dedicated before 550 B.C. the Artemesion was the prime wonder of the classical world. Croesus of Lydia helped to finance it. A father and son team of Knossian architects, Chersiphron and Metagenes, designed it. The temple's 127 marble columns formed double and triple rows close to sixty feet high. They must have created a deep-shadowed virgin forest effect, more than proper to the goddess of the moon and the hunt. As Antipater of Sidon wrote:

"My eyes have looked upon the cliff-like wall of Babylon that chariots can run upon, and on the Zeus by the Alpheus, and the high-hung gardens, and the giant statue of the sun,

and the vast toil of the towering pyramids, and
the huge monument of Mausolis; but when I
saw the House of Artemis soaring into the
clouds, it dimmed those others, and lo! except
in heaven have the sun's eyes never looked on
its like."

In 356 B.C. a man whose express purpose was
to win eternal ill fame (and who shall therefore be
nameless here) destroyed the Artemesion by fire.
A generation later, Alexander the Great offered to
rebuild it. The Ephesians declined the conqueror's
offer on the diplomatic grounds that "it is not fitting
for one deity to build a temple to another." They
themselves reconstructed the Artemesion precisely
as it had been except for a new foundation, or "podium," whose thirteen steps conformed to the ancient lunar calendar. That addition postponed but
could not prevent a second disaster. The sacred
spring at the feet of the goddess kept swelling and
spreading, century by century. It finally became a
marsh, into which the podium subsided and the columns toppled. Then, in A.D. 532, a miraculous resurrection occurred. By order of the Byzantine
Emperor Justinian, Artemis' swamp-grove of fallen
columns was transported to Constantinople. The
entire lot were subsequently incorporated into the
majestic mother of all Christian basilicas and many
an Islamic mosque; namely, the Church of Aghia
Sophia, or "Holy Wisdom."
The colossal statue of Artemis which once graced
the Artemision can be imagined from the famous
copy at the Naples Museum. In her date-palm aspect, as an unshakably mothering presence, Ar-

temis loomed like a petrified tree or breathing column encased in a standing sarcophagus which swarmed with stony animals. Her huge pectoral burden, resembling multiple breasts, was a mass of growing dates. On her head she balanced a heavy shrine containing a meteorite or "stone fallen from Zeus." Her whole hieratic and intensely static image makes a telling contrast to this picture from the pen of the first-ever novelist, Xenophon of Ephesus:

> "The beauty of Anthia moved all to wonder. At fourteen she far surpassed the other girls. Her long, tawny hair was partly braided atop her head but mostly flowing and blowing in the breeze. She wore a small fawn-skin over her knee-length purple chiton. Her weapons were a bow, a quiverful of arrows, a hunting knife, and a spear. Ephesians who happened upon her in the sanctuary of Artemis would often begin to worship, mistaking Anthia for the goddess herself."

If mature, fruitful stillness characterized the statue of Artemis, destructive adolescent freedom was the hallmark of Xenophon's heroine. Yet from the Ephesian viewpoint, as the novelist lets us know, the two figures were practically interchangeable! Only by keeping both in mind can one appreciate the paradoxical spirit of pre-Christian Ephesus. Volatile and yet steady, virginal and yet burgeoning, Artemis reigned over this city for a thousand years. Do modern historians comprehend the goddess? No, nor do I. As this humbling thought occurred to me, I noticed that the cypresses were casting long spearheads of shadow. I had one more place to visit. Could I get there before dark?

Following Jesus' death on the Cross, his mother felt unable to stay in Palestine. Legend relates that John the Beloved Disciple brought Mary to Ephesus and built her a house beside a gushing spring, a mossy source sacred to Artemis, on a mountain overlooking the city. At age sixty-four, Mary was "assumed into heaven" from that secluded refuge— which still exists. Many generations of worms have turned the soil around Mary's dwelling. Sunk in age, the house resembles a low-hunched chapel or hermitage. I arrived there just after sunset. The air was fragrant. The water of the sacred spring was cold and pure to taste.

Turning, I ducked my head to stoop in under the stone lintel of the Virgin's door. The lintel was wider than I thought. Straightening up inside the house I banged my head with a fearful crack against the interior portion of the lintel. My eyes watered; my knees sagged. I felt some dizziness, but not much pain at first. Moving forward in mild shock, I encountered a bronze statue. It was an undistinguished nineteenth-century depiction of Mary. She stood darkly, patiently, embracingly, but without hands. I remembered hearing that her hands had been broken off and lost when some drunken young Turks hurled the statue down a cliff.

A candle stand, with the usual coinbox for contributions, stood by the statue. After inserting a coin, I lit one of the candles. I prayed for my family and others, the quick and the dead. It seemed to me that all my words were falling lifelessly to the floor.

Barely able to stand, I wobbled and swayed. Weird, inchoate anger and grief welled up to suffuse my brain. The candle guttered out, reminding me that I was in no condition to drive back to Kusadasai in the dark, and now my whole head throbbed. Tears came, and I didn't know why. I thought perhaps I ought to kneel down in my loneliness, but then could I get up again? Frightened, I consciously planted my weight on the flagstones, determined to keep my feet and my balance.

Mary extended the hollow stumps of her hands. Invisible fingers touched my heart.

Terror crashed over me and passed like a seventh wave. Pain, grief, anger, washed away. In simple awe, I breathed again. When Mary was not, she was Artemis. And Artemis, being not, is Mary. Although I'd been aware of this in my head, I'd never before grasped its truth. Through the hollow bronze stumps of Mary's hands, meanwhile, fresh understanding flowed into me. It wasn't the Turks who had broken off her hands. Of course not, I did that myself! Strangely, they were my hands, too. Ages ago I had balled my fingers into fists and forgotten to open them again. The fists of my spirit became unclean. I lost then, yet never knew it until now.

Lighting a second candle I gave thanks, and promised to grow new hands.

The first time I visited Jerusalem, the old city or Holy Rock stood within Jordan. Since I was an unpredictable young journalist, the Jordanian Press Office assigned a policeman to look after me. My first request was to visit the Wailing Wall. "Since you're not Jewish," the policeman reluctantly agreed, "we'll go."

The wall had weeds and wildflowers growing between its massive stones. The stone courtyard lay deserted except for some Palestinian children at play. I approached the wall, touched it reverently, bowed my head, and prayed in silence while the policeman stood impatiently by. The children meanwhile interrupted their game to laugh at us. My behavior was totally strange to them. Besides, the policeman and I were both intruding on the children's turf; we'd invaded their make-believe world.

Later we followed the "Via Dolorosa" up winding cobbled streets and steps leading to Mount Moriah's crest. Jesus carried the cross along this route. We passed tourist shops selling plastic crowns of thorns. At the summit the policeman and I removed our shoes and entered the mosque which is called "Al Aqsa."

"The name means 'Far Away,'" he explained. "One night Mohammed the Prophet came to this place in a single moment from a great distance. The Angel Gabriel stood guard over his horse, which was made out of lightning. The Rock itself, this holy Mount Moriah, lifted up to help Mohammed enter heaven. But the Prophet gently put the mountain back down beneath his hand."

Stepping outside again, we went and sat on a low parapet with some blind men. Cypress trees, like black exhalations of the parchment-colored earth, stood over us. "Do you mean to say," I asked the policeman, "the Mount Moriah was alive in Mohammed's time?"

"Oh, yes. It would rear for miles into the sky. By day, its shadow fell on Jericho. By night, a ruby the size of a lion used to shine from here. The Four Rivers of Paradise—Sihon, Bihon, Nile, and Euphrates—flowed from this terrace. The Dome of the Rock which you see over there was pure gold, refined to the point of transparency. All that's changed, but never mind. On Judgment Day, this whole place will be transformed into white coral. For Allah's throne!"

"Will Jesus attend the Last Judgment?"

"No doubt of it. He was a great prophet. Look at that stone cradle. Jesus used to lie in it and prophesy when he was a little baby."

"It's an ancient stone mortar," I said, "for grinding wheat. You may have Jesus mixed up with Adonis, a god of vegetation."

The policeman stiffened, plainly shocked, and pursed his lips. To change the subject I indicated an exquisite small shrine nearby. "And what does that commemorate?"

"The Chain of Truth! If it were still here, we'd soon discover who best understands these matters—you or I." He clutched his pistol holster angrily.

"Concerning these matters," I assured the policeman, "my present understanding is doubtful and intellectual. Yours, on the other hand, is faithful and full-bodied. I respect it. Please continue."

Mollified, the policeman went on: "In King Solomon's time, a blue steel chain hung straight down from Heaven to that shrine. Whoever told the truth could hold onto the chain. Whoever lied would see it fly up out of reach. Solomon seemed wise because he tested each case by the Chain of Truth. So things went on until one day an Arab moneylender came to sue a Jew for nonpayment of debt. The Jew swore up and down that he had already returned the Arab's money. That was true in a sense. He'd concealed the money, for a trick, inside the Arab's walking stick. So the Arab, innocently waving his cane, swore that he'd received nothing."

"One dissembled and the other wasn't thinking," I said. "So what happened?"

"What do you think? Disgusted with them both, the chain flew away forever."

"Well, times change."

"They do, and then again they do not. Underneath us, inside the Rock, is a reservoir called the Cistern of the Leaf. Solomon quarried it out. A man named Shuraik ibn-Habaha went down there once on a routine inspection tour—by boat, naturally. He got lost in the cavern darkness, turned an unexpected corner, and entered the Garden of Paradise! There he remained, for an eternity of bliss."

"How do you know?" I asked.

"Because the moment came when he yearned to revisit Jerusalem. Plucking a leaf from a tree in the Garden, he found himself home once more. Less than a day of Jerusalem time had passed. The leaf which Shuraik ibn-Habasha brought back from the Garden of Paradise never withered."

"What color was it?"

"On top, the red of dried blood interlaced with golden veins. Underneath, black with silver veins. Our wise men identified the leaf as belonging to the Tree of Knowledge. The leaf became the central ornament of the Caliph's treasury, but in time it disappeared."

Australia

The native Australian mythologist Mudrooroo speaks of "earth places that have been sanctified and energized by ancestors in the dreamtime." Mudrooroo's natural science springs from ancestral experience. It holds that such "earth places" are all connected "by the dreaming tracks or song lines like beads scattered along a thread. They have been described as giant batteries which are constantly giving out energy to keep all species strong and ongoing. To destroy them is to destroy some of the earth energy and thus weaken all that live and breathe."

As a widely traveled American with a Judeo-Christian background, I feel the same way about many places and monuments. Stonehenge, Aghia Sophia, and Thomas Jefferson's Monticello, are definitely energizing, each in its degree. Art, literature, and music create "earth places" in one's consciousness. Shakespeare, for example, or Bach. Having filmed Michelangelo's Sistine Ceiling at the Vatican before its tragic, disastrous, "restoration," I believe that to desecrate a masterpiece actually weakens "all that live and breathe." How? By rudely shattering one of the delicate "dreaming tracks" or "songlines" that connect our souls.

In Mudrooroo's lexicon, songlines are specifically "the sound equivalents of the spacial journeys of the ancestors, the lines of which are found also inscribed in aboriginal paintings and carvings. They detail the travels of the ancestors, and each verse may be read in terms of the geographical features of the landscape. Encoded within them are the great ceremonies which reactivate the dreamtime in the present."

The present isn't necessarily easy for pious Aborigines. Consider Mudrooroo's report concerning the central Australian city of Alice Springs:

> "This is the sacred 'djang' place where the caterpillar ancestors of the Mparntwe originated. It was they who formed the landscape around Alice Springs. The caterpillar ancestors came from Anthwerrke and crated the small ridge . . . behind the Desert Palms Motel. Unfortunately this sacred ridge has been desecrated by the municipal authorites; and the road, Barrett Drive, has been renamed Broken Promise Drive by the Arrernte people of Mparntwe to remind them of what happens when the sacred gets in the way of progress."

A stay in the Desert Palms Motel at Alice Springs, in a room with a view of Broken Promise Road, might leave something to be desired. But to hike and camp in a rocky corner of Australia's vastitude with native companions, and listen to their stories around an open fire, would be something else. Conversation, rather than debate, is what we need.

To "converse" means to turn and walk back again, and yet again, like a plowman following his ox as they furrow their field in concert. Aristotle and the "peripatetic philosophers" of classical times consciously practiced this. It's a blissful way to work together, intellectually. Yet so rare today.

Australia's longest river is the Murray, which was dug by a gigantic cod named Otjout in its effort to escape Totyerguil, the primordial hunter. Totyerguil was camping at Swan Hill with his two wives, who were black swans, and their sons. The two boys first noticed Otjout happily basking in a waterhole. They called their father, who came running and hurled a spear into the fish's back. Thrashing mightily, Otjout charged the bank of the waterhole and broke through, creating a foamy channel down the valley.

Totyerguil followed by canoe. Every thirty miles or so, Otjout would pause to rest. Totyerguil caught up each time and hurled another spear. The weapons stuck, forming a spiky ridge along Otjout's back. The fish's descendants still carry that.

Nearing the southern coast, the river which Otjout had made meandered forward through the reeds to mingle its energies with those of the salt sea. Otjout himself had other plans. Plunging straight down, he hid beneath the warm black delta mud.

Totyerguil had thrown all his spears, and lost his prey besides. Disgusted, the great hunter paddled to shore, upended his canoe, and planted it in the riverbank. The canoe grew to be a huge gum tree. Totyerguil also planted his paddle, which became a murray pine. Those trees provide ideal materials for the manufacture of canoes and paddles, respectively.

As for Otjout, he fathered his fish-tribe in the riverbed's bottom mud. Then at midnight he bubbled up, rinsed his silver scales in the strong current, rose with a shrill whistling rush to the surface, broke through, and kept on climbing. His liquidly writhing spirals cast rain in all directions, then grew tight and tighter as he ascended the night sky. He is now the star known as Delphinus.

White is the sacred color of stars and certain Aboriginal ancestors, while black is the color of their dreamtime campfires. Red represents the blood of the giant dog, Marindi, bitten to death by Adno-Arrtina, the wily gecko lizard. Yellow, finally, recalls the markings along the undulant back of Yulunggul, Wagyal, or Arramurrungunji, the many-named rainbow serpent who created rivers galore and still makes thunder and lightning.

The Fortesque River is actually the rainbow serpent's track up from the sea, hollowed out in the dreamtime when he smelled the cooking of something forbidden, namely a ring-necked parrot, an endangered species of considerable charm, which two boys had killed, cleaned, spitted, and set over their campfire to roast.

Slithering swiftly upland, the outraged snake hissed into Gregory Gorge and tunneled thunderously underground. He reemerged to stir the whirlpools in the Pilbara. Then, rearing high through the sky for a long dark moment, he streamed toward the boys' campfire, just as they were commencing supper, and swept them away forever.

Weeping, the boys' families protested that this punishment was really too severe, whereupon the

serpent swirled around again. The people had failed
to get the point. Taboo is taboo; some things are
not done. If the parents were so dimly sentimental
and uncaring of important matters, who would
teach the children? Fanning out like a red-violet
cloak, Yulunggul cast himself suddenly across the
whole region to loose a downpour of torrential violence in which hundreds drowned.

In 1919, a flu epidemic destroyed most of the
central Australian Diyari tribe. This disaster may
have helped persuade a Diyari sharman, or "kunki,"
named Palkalina to reveal certain sacred mysteries.

"The spirit" is present in thunder, black clouds,
dust storms, mirages, desert places, creek beds,
deep woods, hollow trees, serpent forms, and certain frightening bird forms. Kunkis are safe from
the spirit and can deal with him. No one else can.
How does not become a kunki? That requires initiation, plus education, naturally.

One's local kunki is too familiar a figure to do
the initiating, so a kunki from some distant village
or clan is called upon. During the awesome three-
man drama which ensues, the stranger-kunki as-
sumes the role of the spirit. This much we know
thanks to Palkalina's account:

> "I thought that I would get a Kunki to show
> me his art. Our Kunki and I went to a place
> called Tipapilla. There we met a strange Kunki
> who resembled the spirit. When I saw him I
> shivered with great fear. Suddenly the spirit
> disappeared, but returned almost at once. I
> became very hungry. The first day of our se-

clusion in the bush with the spirit he gave me
food, that I have never had before. It was
called kujamara, or spirit's food, which is native tobacco. He then read my thoughts and
saw that I desired to be made a Kunki. He
said that I should not think of other people,
but only of the spirits. I then returned to my
companion, the Kunki. I spoke to him in a
confused manner. He questioned me: 'What
are you?' To which I replied, 'Many spirits.'
He then said, 'You are now a Kunki. In time,
I believe that you will be a good one.' On the
second day I went back into the bush and the
spirit came to me and performed certain rituals, which I learned. I returned to my
companion."

Don't most people have learning experiences of
this sort? At rare moments and in unexpected places
each of us encounters what Palkalina recognized as
"the spirit." However, we tend to dismiss such un-
explainable visitations. They may seem weird in ret-
rospect and strike the reason as having been
unimportant. "I was not myself," one says. But
that's just the point.

It's true that if one's particular experience of spiritual reality occurs in a dream, a state of great stress,
or a drug-induced condition, it has not been earned.
And unearned revelations may prove dangerous in
the extreme. "That way madness lies." But Palkalina well understood—when he returned to his companion after the first day of initiation—that he was
not himself at that point. There was no one to go
crazy, in fact. Palkalina was not so confused as to
fail to realize that he played host to "many spirits"

in momentary transit. Then, too, his companion was there to reassure him: "You are now a Kunki. In time, I believe that you will be a good one."

Palkalina's initiation was already a success, but his education on the spiritual plane was just beginning. On the second day, of course, he went back for specific instruction.

Italy

I feel indebted to well over a hundred sacred places around the globe, where brief encounters between the seeker in myself and the resident spirits have occurred. One such place is the Pantheon in Rome.

For years I lived opposite the church of Santa Dorotea in Trastevere, a short walk from the Pantheon. I often strolled across the Ponte Sisto to visit the monument. It nestles, like some gray, forbidding tortoise of tremendous size, stuck in a maze of winding little streets between Piazza navona and the Corso. Scores of stray cats inhabit the bricked excavation trench around part of its base. Sixteen smooth stone columns, each one fourteen feet around and forty-one feet high, carry its austere portico. Its huge bronze doors are the originals, believe it or not. Some seventy generations, so far, have passed between them.

The circular interior stands wide open, like a carved-out boulder of dim-colored conglomerate. One hardly notices the altar niche or the statuary and entablatures around the walls; those things merely fringe the bone-bareness of the enormous central area: a petrified half-bubble as it were, 142 feet in diameter. This truly vast room is capped by a dome at the apex of which—142 feet above the floor—hovers a thirty-foot-wide circular aperture filled with sky. One feels like a tiny, incipient thought adrift in the open-topped cranium of some newborn baby.

Admiral Agrippa, who defeated Antony and Cleopatra in the naval battle of Actium, dedicated the Pantheon in the year 27 B.C. The Emperor Hadrian restored it about A.D. 110. And then, in 609, Pope Boniface IV reconsecrated the perfectly preserved structure as the Church of St. Mary of the Martyrs. It now contains the tombs of various kings and queens, along with that of a serene Renaissance master: Raphael.

Originally, the Pantheon's seven interior niches held statues of the deities who presided over the days of the week, namely the sun god Apollo, the moon goddess Diana, and the planets Mars, Mercury, Jupiter, Venus, and Saturn—in that order. So the whole thing was a sort of spiritual gyroscope, an open locus at which to recognize and revere the guiding forces of the spacetime continuum. Thanks to the abstracting genius of its planners and builders, the Pantheon still offers that possibility. Nathaniel Hawthorne sensed it when he wrote:

> "The great slanting beam of sunshine was visible all the way to the pavement, falling upon motes of dust or a thin smoke of incense imperceptible in shadow. Insects were playing to and fro in the beam, high up toward the

opening. There is a wonderful charm in the naturalness of all this; one might fancy a swarm of cherubs coming down through the opening and sporting in the broad ray."

I have a confession to make. Once on a bitterly cold winter day, I forgot-on-purpose to remove my hat in the Pantheon. The priest in charge felt it his duty to remind me that, after all, we were in church. He used body language alone, with gentle Roman fluency. Bowing in my direction, the priest discreetly pointed to his tonsure; that is, the shaved spot at the top of his head which marked him as belonging to a monastic order. Then, straightening again, he glanced smilingly up at the bronze-lipped aperture high overhead.

I got the message. In approaching the spiritual world, open-mindedness is not enough. Mindful openness works better. Since then I always take my hat off in the Pantheon—which takes its own hat off to the sun, the moon, and the turning stars.

"By ordering the heavens," Plato explains in the *Timaeus,* "the Creator made an everlasting image, moving according to number, of the eternity which abides in unity. This image is what we call time. Before the birth of heaven there were no days, nights, months, or years."

From 700 to 300 B.C. the ancient Etruscan city-states dominated central Italy. Their wealth came from trade and the iron mines on the island of Elba. Like their Minoan ancestors, the Etruscans were gluttons for sex and celebration. They had a wonderful time, apparently, until the first roman legions came clanking along to crush their revels flat. Rome had a new civilization to build, and that was that.

"Because a fool kills a nightingale with a stone, is he therefore greater than the nightingale? Because the Roman took the life out of the Etruscan, was he therefore greater than the Etruscan?" These eloquently rhetorical questions were posed by D. H. Lawrence. Writing under Mussolini's dictatorship, Lawrence made clear where his own sympathies lay.

Driving out of Rome at dawn one day I bowled smoothly north with low hills on my right and the flat Maremma plain stretching to the seashore on my left. The morning turned pink and gold before I curved off the highway onto a blacktop road winding gently up into the hills. Soon I reached the pink stucco gatehouse to Cerveteri's archeological site: an Etruscan necropolis. No guards, guides, or tourists had yet arrived, and so I strolled straight in alone.

There were hundreds of grave mounds, bubbling up in clumps among the dark umbrella pines, oaks, cypresses, and mulberry trees whose blossoms hung murmurous with honeybees. The mounds themselves, largely overgrown with grass and wildflowers, were beehive shaped. Some stood house-high, while others kept low profiles. Houseflies, dragonflies, and an extraordinary variety of butterflies kept darting and hovering about. Stone moldings protruded from the turf at the base of each mound. Archways of cantilevered stones surmounted the entrance steps leading down into dark burial chambers. In the sandy soil amid outcroppings of bedrock tufa, innumerable ants constructed tiny imitations of the tombs themselves.

A small stone house or "ark," thought to represent the female sex, used to stand outside each tomb. Also, a stone phallus, set in a tuifa socket. When D. H. Lawrence passed this way, he noted that "Etruscan consciousness was rooted quite blithely in these symbols." Contemporary consciousness is less than blithe, so every ark and phallus has since been spirited away from the necropolis to stand on dusty shelves in museum basements "for study purposes."

Coming to a large mound-cluster I leaped a sky-colored puddle, turned right, and climbed a rock-cut flight of steps. At the top was a breezeless hollow with only the tender blue sky for company. I was about to climb a second flight leading off to the left when I noticed two stalks of grass lying across it in such a way as to form an "X." Instinct told me not to step over that. Instead, I followed a muddy pathway which led up and around to the entrance of the highest mound. From its cantilevered archway, ten feet ahead of me, voices came. I stood motionless, trying to make them out. I felt no fear as yet, only intense surprise.

Bees? Cave swallows? No, the sounds were human. I counted four, possibly five, male and female voices drifting amiably up out of the tomb. The language was strange to me. I felt that I was eavesdropping, outside of time itself, one someone else's roof. What if I were to move forward and look down the stairs into the tomb chamber? Would I glimpse a small banquet hall, with friends reclining together as in ancient days, sipping from wide-brimmed winecups? The prospect was crazy, awesome. I had to see.

The moment I leaped across to the head of the stairs, the voices fell silent. Crouching, I peered down a dozen steps to an interior stone doorway, wider at the top than at the bottom. Beyond the doorway: blackness, nothing more. Retreating hastily, I listened once again for the voices. There were none; my heart sank like a stone.

As a mother cat transports a kitten between her teeth, silence held me motionless by the neck. The whole world stood on tiptoe to greet someone I knew but could not see. Then, with her familiar smile, she came lightly dancing down and around the dim tomb-chamber of my cranium. The tomb-chamber with its black forest of easels, its turpentine tang, and rain thrumming the skylight. Softly she stepped down, down into my midmind. The sun slanted warmly upon my back, yet I stood among sweeping shadows: smoke upon the wind. So smoky-soft her hair when it was long. Her kiss resembled a fine desert wine, a "mavro-daphne." Yes, memories may burn and burn without ever being consumed.

Doesn't suicide rank right after cancer as a prime cause of death in America? I've known nearly a dozen suicides. Both of the women whom I most loved in youth destroyed themselves later on. They were sexy, brilliant, fun-loving, original people, neither of whom cared whether school kept or not. They weren't guilt-ridden, nor did they feel especially beholden to the world. They did fear death, as who does not. And yet these women ran, ran, with arms flung wide, into death's cold comfort. Why? It's true, as Wordsworth said, that most of us come "trailing clouds of glory" into the world.

Soon, however, each one's luminous path frays downward to overhang an awesome nullity. Like mist a mile deep, the future falls away beneath our feet. Haven't we all felt that? And haven't most of us, including me, flirted with suicide?

But those women weren't flirting; they were dead.

With thumping heart, I fled the empty scene. Five minutes later I found myself sitting on a boulder in the shade of a giant oak which overhung a tomb having a padlocked gate: "Closed for repairs." I rested, nearly motionless, for some time. Wrens, blackcaps, house sparrows, European robins, and a single goldfinch stopped by to keep me company. They may also have helped me understand what had occurred. I'd unwittingly surprised a team of peasant tomb robbers. The part-time bandits spoke Italian, of course, but in their own thick local dialect. The moment my shadow blocked the sunlight at the top of the stairs the freelancers naturally fell silent—holding their breath in shock, no doubt— and doused their lights.

I listened hopefully for nightingales, but there were none. The stillness of a greenish black lizard caught my eye. He flicked his forked tongue at me as if to say: "Live in the present!"

By noon I was driving northward again to visit another major tomb site, at Tarquinia. There an archeological student in faded blue jeans and a maroon sweater offered to show me around. The necropolis had recently yielded a harvest of wheat. Sweet-scented chamomile grew along the borders of the stubble. Grave beyond his years, my guide strode ahead, swinging his lantern with a determined air. We walked considerable distances to scramble down into the widely scattered tombs, which still had fresco murals intact. The frescoes depicted columns, beams, and hanging garlands which framed picture-window views of uninhibited lovemaking, drinking, feasting, swimming, racing, juggling, instrumental music, and dancing above all.

These images must have been painted in partial darkness—with the help, I imagine, of sunbeams narrowly bounced from bronze mirrors down the tomb shafts. The artists had to work fast in order to finish before the plaster dried on the tomb walls. Hence mistakes went uncorrected, details were not filled in, and soft edges prevailed. Charcoal, ivory, dried blood, turquoise, olive, and sun-yellow were the predominant colors. Where one hue closed out along a contour, another began as if taking up a conversation. Freshness, spontaneity, and rhythmic execution characterized every painting. All were clearly done to give the beloved dead a happy reprise of life beneath the scorched blue breast of the open sky.

My guide had saved the famous "Tomb of the Baron" for last. Emotionally drained by my long day, I didn't know if I felt up to it. He insisted, however, promising that I would not regret making the effort. Removing his sunglasses and switching on his lantern one last time, he descended a final underground flight of stairs ahead of me. Now his electric beam revealed a nobly erect woman in profile. Two youths approached her, one from either side, leading beautiful, eager horses. One horse was red, the other black. The woman posed lightly, yet with columnar solidity, between the two animals. She gazed across her lifted veil at the black horse. The black horse represented death, my guide remarked. The red one stood for life. With a somber and somehow proprietary frown, he assured me that we were in this woman's tomb, watching her opt for death. This standard "explanation" barely interrupted my reverie. It held no relevance to what I experienced.

Nothing was "represented" in the fresco; nothing separated me from the noble figure there. I was "she." As for the horses, they were too slim for riding purposes. However, they would make a springly chariot team. The rust-red horse pranced with life; the shadow-black horse did the same.

Ireland and the Rest of the World

On a secluded beach in Donegal, where Colum Cille was born, my children and I were fooling with a soccer ball. From the dunes a tall youth arose, shouting that we disturbed his rest. I asked what his name might be.

"William Reilly Colum!" he called out; adding after a moment: "Billy to me friends."

Invited to join our game, Billy cheerfully did so. Our shouts drew other fellows from along the shore, and we soon had a good one going: "All Ireland versus the Rest of the World." Twice, Billy knocked me flat. My nine-year-old daughter meanwhile delivered the winning goal for the Rest of the

World. Either she outran our new friend, or else he delicately permitted her to slip past.

We were staying at a country inn, but Billy slept "rough" on the beach. He consumed quantities of ale, lay around in the sun, and swam from time to time.

"Oi'm discontented," he explained. "Me old man operates a pig farm over east in Meath. Himself commanded me to drive our fattest animals across the border into Northern Ireland and sell them for a good price there. I got a better price than Himself ever need know about. So I ambled down the coast here with money in me pocket and no hurry in me head. I have to go on home, but first I'll content my heart a little. Understand?"

"I do," I said. "But beware the sow in the sea!"

"Eh? Who's she?"

"A sort of oversoul. She's mourning for her children, and she bristles with resentment there beneath the waves."

Billy punched my shoulder in his muscle-numbing way. "I know pigs better than mesel'," he said. "Sure and if I meet the old sow in swimming, I'll crack her acrost the snout with a conch shell."

And into he surf he ran.

The next evening, on the Fourth of July, Billy joined us for a picnic atop a low hill crowned with a Druid burial monument or *cromlech*. This consisted of three mossy boulders standing upright, and a massive stone slab laid across them like a low roof. Sitting on the cromlech's seaward side, we watched the sun hesitantly descending while we ate. Then I clambered up on top of the cromlech to propose a toast and lead a couple of songs. At that point some thirty cows assembled from along the sloping pasture. They closed in threateningly, plainly resenting the presence of our group.

"It's all right, kids. Daddy will talk to them!"

So said my life-partner, Jane Winslow Eliot, reassuring everyone except myself. Planting my feet more firmly on the great stone, I straightened up and made a large pushing gesture with my hands. The cows paused, then spread out to form an orderly semicircle. With that achieved, I earnestly addressed the animal and human assembly. I offered them the legend of Billy's namesake: Colum Cille. Without so much as a "Moo!" everyone heard my story through. When it was over the cows shook their heads thoughtfully and ambled away. I was astonished at my own prowess, until Billy assured me that it was only natural. Every farmer knows, he said, that cows relish the sound of the human voice.

On the morning after our picnic, I wandered down to the beach to greet the sunrise. Billy Colum was already awake and anxiously heaping driftwood on his campfire. "Will you be boiling up some tea?" I asked.

"It's not that, bucko. I'm afeared of the mist!"

By noon he was gone. Later on, I got a long-distance call: "It's me! I'm back home with the pigs. Can ye smell them?"

"Of course."

"Well, now then!"

"Now then!" There was a pause.

"What will ye do without me, foin fool that ye are?"

I told Billy that I planned to take long walks in the poet William Butler Yeats' footsteps. Carrowmore, Beltra Strand, Ballisodare glittering between its hayfields, Sleuth Wood, the brown salmon stream down by the Salley Gardens, Dromohaire, the Lake Isle of Innisfree, Glen Carr the swan-frequented lake, bare Ben Bulden, Drumcliffe, and Knocknarea were on my list.

"That whole country is gentle," Billy said on the phone. "I mean it's haunted by night and by day. Who was it, once again, ye're after followin'? A poet, did ye say? Sounds more like a warlock, considerin' the territory."

"I'll be all right. We're in the midst of life, and there's nothing but life."

"It's a strange thing ye're telling me now!"

"I'm quoting Yeats. He implied that death does not exist. I half believe it, Billy, but if only my heart knew!"

"Well, may the better sort of devils guide your footsteps anyhow. And be careful, bucko."

Like religion, the arts also have their saints. The Irish Renaissance of a century ago revived the spiritual brio and half-angry gallantry of early Christian Eire. George Bernard Shaw was a second Saint Patrick, for example. James Joyce was Longarad Whitefoot all over again. And William Butler Yeats reoccupied Colum Cille's crystal throne.

The air hums with numberless spirits. One couldn't put the point of a knife between the ghosts surrounding our lives, so thickly do they swarm. Yeats knew this; he practiced occult magic and spirit communication constantly, while milking verbal music from the mares of night. "A tattered coat upon a stick," he called himself. Yes, but with emeralds and pearls in the pockets, precipitations of the ineffable.

In youth, Yeats lived near Knocknarea. In age, he often revisited the region. The name Knocknarea derives from Irish for "hill of Sacrifice." Yeats must have climbed the hill at least a dozen times. When I left the road out of Sligo to walk up the hill in my turn, three dogs barked. One of them was black and lacked a tail. He followed me for a while.

The slope which rose before me was dedicated to a Celtic nature-goddess known as Maeve. She had a mare's head on a human body, or sometimes the reverse. Maeve's first husband was Llyr the mumbling one, the long, gray, fructifying sea-wind. Among their numberless children were fairy creatures, and animals as well. Maeve herself had various names and many different lives. Five thousand years ago she reigned over Ireland as Cessair. Her daughter Circe was the sorceress who befriended Odysseus. Then, in the year of Jesus' birth, Maeve incarnated as a human being. Later she assumed fairy form as "Queen Mab" of the Little People.

My walk wound upward between low stone walls. Overlays of gray-green lichen gave the stones a living, transparent look. A donkey blocked my way for a few minutes while munching a pathside lunch. Purple thistles dangled from the animal's gray lips.

Bluebottle flies inhabited the windless dips. Buzzing, they bit my face and hands. It struck me that people maneuver by turns and progress by contraries: left foot, right foot. Sometimes we feel split down the middle. But in point of fact we are nondichotomous, meandering complete through each and every moment of existence. By means of a continuous, unconscious, interchange of energies which do not belong to us, we register and affect everything—in all directions. The private worlds within ourselves and the agreed-upon world "out there" constitute a single seamless reality.

A friendly brown mare nodded to me from a windy gate. My breath was getting shorter as the horizon enlarged. The harebells, raspberry bushes, and daisies adorning the lower stretch gave way to heather. Like tiny sky-cups the heather blossoms poured libations on the sea-wind. I gazed down upon tilted pastures, like patches on a beggar's cloak, crawling with goats.

Maeve's Cairn—her house-high mound of cloud-colored rocks—nipples the crest of Knocknarea. It has been excavated more than once, but not a single rag or bone relic of Maeve's many lives was ever found under the stones. When I arrived at the base of the cairn I found to my surprise that I was not alone. A hunched, swart figure sat perched on the cairn's crest, squinting down at me through steel-rimmed spectacles. In plain imitation of the poet Yeats, he wore a broad-brimmed black hat plus a flowing black tie.

I waved, but the figure did not respond. Annoyed, curious, both at once, I scrambled up the cairn to confront him. Loose stones made the footing insecure; I had to watch my step. When I reached the top and raised my eyes, no one was there! Panting, I peered around and down. No one.

Gray vastness, with some green and blue showing through, surrounded me. the seacoast cut and curved below as if to parry the mumbling god's cavalry: white-maned horses of the sea. In the distance lay calm, silvery Lough Gill. Southward the Wild Ox Mountains tossed their cloudy horns. The whole sweep of earth, air, and sky washed my bewilderment away. Sitting down where the poet had appeared to perch, I laughed with happiness.

When I travel, what comes toward me already contains everything I bring to that which I shall meet. Thus an apparition—or better, a visitation—will sometimes occur. It soon vanishes, and that's to the good. Discovery beats possession any day. Imaginative participation is more valuable than passive faith. There is always a greater present moment than I know about.

Vision and Chaos, that shapeless but respectable divine couple, were upset. It seemed to them that the Serene Monarch of the Universe never made a mistake. From their viewpoint this was highly improper. It made Vision see red and Chaos churn within. These intimate activities resulted in the birth of their son: an ugly, cheery little fellow known as "Dwarf." No sooner had he come of age than Dwarf sought and received an audience with the Serene Monarch. "I'm the person of least account in all the world," Dwarf complained. "I have nothing on earth to call my own. My request is modest. Grant me as much of your kingdom as I can cover in a hop, skip, and jump!"

Smiling indulgently, the Serene Monarch nodded. "Right, little man. Show us your prowess and you shall have your wish."

Dwarf's hop swept like flame from pole to pole of the planet. his skip ranged like lightning around the upper air. His jump encircled the sun itself. In a trice, Dwarf stood once again before the Serene Monarch—who sat nonplussed for a long moment.

"If I were to have granted you permanent possession," the Serene Monarch decided at last, "I would have made a mistake, which is impossible. So let's just say you did possess this planet plus the sun and a considerable space in between, for an instant of time. Congratulations! After this exploit, no one will ever again regard you as a person of small account."

Divine in Hindu lore, "Dwarf" also speaks to our humanity. We're small, all right. But imagination, too, hops, skips, and jumps when and where it will. Imagination shakes hands with the stars. Stranger still, imagination can even slip inside another person's mind—momentarily, at least. Imagination is a power that all of us possess. But in so-called adulthood most people allow it to wither away through undernourishment and disuse. Don't let this happen in your case! That's my one plea.

A dimension may exist where in particles communicate by radiating photons which possess no mass whatsoever yet leap from here to the Andromeda galaxy and back again with insatiable speed—like Dwarf in the Hindu myth. First proposed by John Cramer in 1986, this interaction involved numberless simultaneous "handshakes" taking place to weave, unweave, thread, and re-thread an electromagnetic spacetime labyrinth—a silent music of the smallest spheres there are.

Cramer's mathematical "field of interaction at a distance" is not a place that I'm equipped to enter, but ignorance of higher mathematics would be a poor excuse for not enjoying fresh ideas. Then, too, I've had the pleasure of pacing out more than a dozen North European labyrinths, some in open fields and others on cathedral floors. I've seen the unexpected on Maeve's Cairn, I've been laughed at beside the Wailing Wall, and instructed to remove my hat in the Pantheon. Along the way I've learned something about Sefwi magic, Aboriginal song-lines, Turtle's ambitions, and Spider's secrets. I even know the name of Grandfather Sky's daughter. So do you, for that matter. Although such materials and experiences are less neat than mathematical demonstrations, they belong to the same world of human imaginative endeavor. So my travels and mythological studies have helped to prepare me for the "theory" which Cramer offers.

"Cramer's interpretation is very much a myth for our times," says science writer John Gribbin. "It is easy to work with and to use in constructing mental images of what is going on, and with any luck at all it will supersede the Copenhagen Interpretation as the standard way of thinking about quantum physics for the next generation of scientists."

The Copenhagen Interpretation of quantum physics was largely the work of Niels Bohr, Werner Heisenberg, and Max Born. If this classic concept no longer seems adequate, the present academic approach to mythology is also impractical. At best, mythology is treated as a subtext of anthropology, psychology, literature, and art. At worst, it's regarded as a soft refuge for neurotic scholars, wishful poets, and the vaguely unbright. The time has arrived to broaden our perspective on this subject. In fact, myth underlies everything we know and surrounds all that we can become.

Science requires proofs, religion requires faith, and philosophy requires discrimination. Mythology lays the foundation for all three. This is possible because mythology consists of significant stories that have been developed and redeveloped by many, many members of the human race. Not only that, but also listened to with rapt, participating attention in every corner of human spacetime. Storytellers speak from imagination, storylisteners hear with imagination. To actively participate in this process is a free act which leads to an expanded kind of freedom.

But this freedom isn't necessarily easy. Although freighted with memory, insight, and wisdom, sacred myth also shakes and shudders with insoluble mysteries. When you return a caged wild animal to the wilderness it will have much to learn and to suffer. The same is true here. Like quantum physics, mythology also is a "senseless" and therefore difficult discipline. Its goal is to arrive at a "unified field" by creating the broadest possible basis of knowledge and sympathy, plus an abiding hunger for significance, within ourselves.

Of all the sacred places in the world, the most important is your heart. When you devote yourself to the study of myth with reverent curiosity and care, it will promote the sharp, even painful, budding of wonder there—so that discrimination, faith, and proof may flower.

PART ONE

The Magic
of the
Mythosphere

Introduction

Timeless myths play into everybody's personal time zone. One thing that all of us have wrestled with is the inevitability of death and the brevity of any single life. Historically, our species has devoted enormous effort to confronting this and "working it out" in various forms, whether religious, philosophical, or mythological. The Christian "Heaven" is one example. Plato's "World of Ideas" is another. To dismiss all such concepts out of hand would be painfully provincial. The "prove it" attitude impoverishes imagination and stultifies discussion. On the other hand, both reason and imagination are empowered by open-minded reverence for the intellectual and imaginative legacy which our ancestors created and preserved for us.

Myth is a major portion of that legacy.

You're sitting at a cafe table in Piazza San Marco, Venice, sipping an espresso. The sky overhead is half sapphire and half pewter, wet and dry. Soon the bronze giants atop the clock tower—"La Torre dell' Orologio"—will rouse themselves to strike the hour upon a bell standing twice their own height. The giants have been doing this, with wonderful and faithful resonance, since 1499.

The broad blue-and-gold clock face lower down is decorated with signs of the zodiac. The minute hand keeps moving from one starry realm to another. Predictability is the pavement beneath our feet. Most things happen as expected; that's the miracle of every day.

Meanwhile Venice herself, all hands agree, is slowly subsiding into the sea. Subject to time's unimaginable touch, this loveliest of cities must drown. Venice will join the entourage of Okeanos, the all-encircling ocean deity who rides a mother-of-pearl chariot pulled by paired hippocamps and plumed with spermy spume. Laughing, Okeanos shakes a coral trident. His white beard streams sideways, glittering.

Early in the nineteenth century, William Wordsworth wished he were "a Pagan suckled in a creed outworn." The poet yearned for "glimpses that would make me less forlorn." He longed to "hear old Triton blow his wreathed horn." About a century later, T. S. Eliot implied that he himself had "heard the mermaids singing, each to each." But, he added ruefully: "I do not think that they will sing to me."

This old lament from the Isle of Man tells how things are for most of us at some level of consciousness:

> O that a great wind would blow that I might hear from my love, and that she might come to me over the high mountains; we would meet each other beside the shore. Gladly, gladly would I go to meet her, if I knew my love was there; O gladly, gladly would I sit

down beside her with my arm as a pillow to
her under her head.

That's the crux of the matter. If one has no confidence in the voice of love upon the wind, no belief
in the summons of the deep, and no courage to
follow Triton's horn or join in the mermaids' song,
nothing further can happen.

Yes, there goes the great bell of La Torre dell'
Orologio. Its brilliant bonging jolts one's thoughts
away from legend, into history.

One day during the latter part of the sixth century B.C., an Ionian Greek named Pythagoras
paused to listen at the door of a bronze foundry.
The sound of hammering on the anvil struck him
as musical. Each separate hammer sounded a note
of its own. Stepping inside the foundry, he observed that the hammer handles were of different
lengths. Pythagoras thought about that. He did
some measuring and calculating. It wasn't long before a totally fresh and mathematically elegant perspective lay open before him. Structure and
vibration, he proclaimed, play crucial roles in
music.

He left out the time-dimension, whose time had
not yet come. Like all of his contemporaries, Pythagoras regarded time as being a leisurely spin-
motion manifested by the passage of seasons, the
phases of the moon, and the distant yet precisely
repeated circling of starry bodies. The constellation
known as the Pleiades was especially important not
only to the ancient Greeks but to our ancestors
around the world. That's because the Pleiades mark
the onset of summer and winter by their rising and

setting. Pythagoras called those stars "the harp of the Muses" upon which celestial music is played.

Ouroborus, the milky night-dragon who chases her own tail from aeon to aeon, seemed to surround and guard all things. Now, if Ouroborus is not an actuality, neither is time in the abstract.

In the abstract, time is a dotted line; where each dot represents the ghost of a departed or an unborn quantity. This line won't stop, not even for our dearest treasure. Namely, the present moment. Mathematics needs no such experiential ground. Nor does physics, the armature of scientific myth.

It so happens that during Pythagoras' lifetime the Hellenic world lay open to a rich an fabulous intellectual infusion. This came chiefly from Zoroastrian Persia, but distant India also contributed. Oxford classicist M. L. West has eloquently summarized the result:

> In some ways one might say that it was the very extravagance of oriental fancy that freed the Greeks from the limitations of what they could see with their own eyes: led them to think of ten-thousand-year cycles instead of human generations, of an infinity beyond the visible sky and below the foundations of the earth, of a life not bounded by womb and tomb but renewed in different bodies aeon after aeon. It was now that they learned to think that good men and bad have different destinations after death; that the fortunate soul ascends to the luminaries of heaven; that God is intelligence; that the cosmos is one living creature; that the material world can be analyzed in terms of a few basic constituents

such as fire, water, earth, metal; that there is a world of Being beyond perception, beyond time. These were conceptions of enduring importance for ancient philosophy. This was the gift of the Magi.

The questions and possibilities which the Wise Men of the ancient East proposed are splendidly illustrated by legends the world over. Here's one:

Dionysius the Areopagite ("Saint Denys" in France) found martyrdom at the age of a hundred and ten. He was decapitated. This occurred beside the Seine River in Paris. Afterward, Dionysius got up from his knees and stood swaying. He thought the situation over for a long minute. Raised in the pagan faith of his Athenian ancestors, counseled by his partner Damaris, converted to Christianity by Saint Paul, harried through all the Roman provinces to Gaul, and finally condemned to death by imperial decree, the old man had much to recall.

Bending down, he retrieved his head from the ground.

"Nothing of importance," his head remarked, "requires or rewards subservience to Caesar; or to God either. Why should God take the slightest interest in subservience? Instead, the deity suggests that you climb up on your two feet, stretch out your two hands, and freely join with that which draws you in spirit. Sisters and brothers, ancestors, and descendants too, are waiting to play with you."

Cradling the wise head in his arms, Dionysius turned away from the river. He passed through Sword Alley, the cobbled Street of Prostitutes, and on up the broad Beggars' Staircase. Trailed by the wondering Paris throng, Dionysius carried his head all the way up to the summit of Montmartre.

There on the open hilltop, gratefully, the saint gave up the ghost.

Skeptical people search for "scientific certainties," while people of faith keep their eyes upon "eternal verities." But religion is unprovable science, and science is unacknowledged religion. Between them they cause deserts to bloom. They make cities rise. Then these twin rivers fall in tumult, threading the primordial abyss. Finally reborn in legendary form they reappear. Thus Animism, Shamanism, Pantheism, Paganism, Taoism, Gnosticism, Witchcraft, Alchemy, Astrology, and so on, shimmer lightly up and down the peripheries of contemporary consciousness. As the Aurora Borealis trails its brilliant veils around the northern hemisphere, so ancient science and old-time religion play about us, now and forever.

Two thousand years after Pythagoras, during the fifteenth century of our era, town clocks became common throughout Europe. People learned to live by the clock. Thus linear time—the kind that flies forward rather than around and around—first imbued human consciousness. Then, toward the end of the sixteenth century, along came Galileo. He was first to realize that the only way to comprehend the physics or material dynamics of bodies in motion is to time them.

The year that Galileo died, Sir Isaac Newton was born. Along with Leibniz, Newton invented calculus, upon which higher mathematics is based. Using this tool, humanity has since gained a broad comprehension of physics—itself a human invention. Our so-called "known universe" displays a nighttime radius of some ten billion light-years. Contrastingly its keystone component—that damned elusive "top quark"—existed for a trillionth of a trillionth of a second, once upon a time. So states contemporary myth.

Meanwhile, Benjamin Franklin's prophecy has proved to be self-fulfilling. "Time is money," and "man-hours" are routinely bought and sold. With hardly a thought, people trade these pearls for peanuts. We'll even lay down our lives, purely in a business way. That is, upon the economic chopping block.

It's strange. One steps into the whirling of the stars on little clay feet. One labors for so many thousand hours and then "retires"; after which the world hurls one out again, stumps first. Or so it seems when our concept of linear time crumples up against the ancient cyclical sort. But life need not be all that brutish, brief, and cruel.

What is time? The cyclical idea still seems emotionally right. It's a heart-comforting vision which the night sky corroborates. But the linear view of time is far more satisfactory to the mind. This accords with the vast majority of near-at-hand physical facts perceived by us. Since there is irreconcilable conflict between the cyclical perspective and the linear one, most moderns choose the latter and go comfortless. That's not good enough. The very act of making such a choice implies that only two possible perspectives on this extremely mysterious subject exist.

Friedrich Nietzsche described our continuing dilemma in "The Birth of Tragedy" (1887):

> Man today, stripped of myth, stands famished amongst all his pasts and must dig frantically for roots, be it among the most remote antiquities. What signifies our great historical hunger, our clutching about us of countless other cultures, our consuming desire for knowledge, if not the loss of myth, of a mythic home, a mythic womb?

Yet never does the "mythic womb" disappear. Far-distant although near at hand, intimate and unfathomable, is the object of our desire. It's natural that we yearn, but there's no need for despair.

In fourteenth-century Normandy, the Cistercian prior Guillaume de Digulleville had a vision. His soul entered Paradise and saw "the King" seated on a throne "brighter than the sun," surrounded by a corona of precious gems. Nearby sat "the Queen," urgently conversing with her husband from a round throne of smoky quartz.

Doesn't Guillaume's vision reflect the actual relation between Earth and Sun? Impregnated and fed by the mighty influx of sun fire, this watery-skinned, richly steaming crystal planet of ours both creates and nurtures life. So it's only natural that myths around the globe conjure forth Father Sun and Mother Earth time after time.

Mystic visions and primal myths are only the beginning. Folktales, fairytales and legends follow. As the sparkling of diamonds, rubies, and emeralds delight the eyes, so this treasurehouse of stories contains the power to bemuse and excite one's own imagination. Every now and then, one finds a story which speaks to and confirms one's own happiest dreams. For example, here's a tale about a summer night in Kansas not so long ago:

The stars were shining brightly when a slim, yellow-haired maiden slipped into the lonely farmer's bed. Although he'd never seen her before in all his life, the farmer well understood that he had always adored her. So they enjoyed each other's company, blissfully entwined, until the break of dawn. Then without a word—yet with a long backward look in the semidarkness—the maiden disappeared.

Wonderingly, the farmer arose. Pulling on his blue jeans and clodhopper boots, he blinked away his tears. Stepping outside, he went to take a look at his glistening green cucumber patch. Behind the farmer's broad naked back, meanwhile, the sun swam up over the horizon. The sun was swiftly journeying on its long way westward out of Asia, Europe, the Atlantic Ocean, and on over the United States. Bearded with brilliant rays the sun advanced, drinking the dews of night.

Along the western edge of the cucumber patch, thirty-three sunflowers stood blooming. Gracefully they bowed in the farmer's direction. Dewdrops glistened upon all but one. Somehow that single flower had found refuge from the foggy, nocturnal dew. But where?

The farmer guessed the answer. Marching boldly up to the solitary dry sunflower, he gently caressed its yellow corona of petals. Softly, the farmer pressed his lips to the dark, dry-seed spiral at the blossom's core. At that moment the birds began to sing. The dewless sunflower changed into a yellow-haired maiden once again.

Permanently, this time, for he'd come to her.

The vast continuum of whispers, songs, thunder-heads, bright sunshine, deities, monsters, altars, distances, titans, philosophic palaces, and astonishing discoveries upon which "Mind" depends—does all this nestle inside my skull? Personal experience says otherwise. Thinking, dreaming, and imagining go on and on without even starting to cram one's cranium. Mental furniture flies freely in and out, like breathing. Why? Because one's intellectual doors and windows stand wide open to an infinitely greater area.

I call this the mythosphere.

Imagine a cathedral rose-window of garnet and lapis lazuli, transmogrified into prismatic, luminous, leisurely twirling skeins. The mythosphere is just such a legend-globe. Her mingled mysteries and clarities swirl about us, light-years higher, aeons wider, than your brain or mine. We can't leap out of nature, nor do we exit the mythosphere. It's only natural for us to cherish, explore and enjoy home-territory. Every man, woman, and child on earth has a soul-right to the mythosphere's sun-warm orchard and her attic trunks crowded with curious delights. We're not exploiters, outsiders, students, or tourists either, in the mythosphere. We're home.

"What distinguishes mythologist Alexander Eliot's 'mythosphere' from psychologist Carl Gus-

tave Jung's 'collective unconscious'?" Recently a
colleague wrote to ask me that. Grateful for the
query, I replied that psychologists and mythologists
alike owe a lot to Jung, but we need to break out
of the deterministic spell that he so grandly cast.
Not "archetypes" but archepassions drive mythology, religion, and the arts. Love, for one thing.
Anger, for another. Anger plays volcanically
through Jehovah, thunderously through Zeus, and
rather squeakily through me on occasion. It's part
of the mythospheric weather-system.

The mythosphere, as I define this, is by no means
confined to the unconscious. Nor is it inhabited by
changeless archetypes. The mythosphere spins on
its own, embracing and nurturing each person's intellectual freedom.

Nobody has mapped the entire territory, let
alone analyzed it. The mythosphere is too vast and
changeable for that. As humanity continues its own
creation so the mythosphere evolves; changing,
adding, enriching all the time. It might be likened
to an ocean-size bubble wherein our thoughts play
about like golden carp in green waters.

With all the grabbing that's done, there aren't
enough material goods to go around. Division has
a major role in practical life, and greed impoverishes. But there's no way to wound, rip, dissect, or
strip the mythosphere. The fruits of her cornucopia
are here to be shared. Not just for the joy of it; we
can help them multiply. So let's partake! Imagina-
tively at least; creatively at best.

If that sounds difficult, remember it's an age-old
human power. Even children partake of the mythosphere. I'll go further. Some of us so-called adults

gaze back upon a time when we felt intimately connected, in our wide-eyed way, to the mythospheric mystery drama. I mean, before parents and teachers rang down the curtain to "explain" what we had seen.

Young Rain

In the beginning was a story, and inside the story was a beginning, and so on, without end. Consider this very ancient Indo-Chinese myth, which survives in at least seven widely differing versions:

First came Lord Thunder, then a lightning-crack, and out stepped Lo Kuo. He built himself a palace of banana leaves, but soon Lord Thunder rolled along and stamped it down. Angered, Lo Kuo transformed Lord Thunder into a rooster. He put it in a cage. "Give me water," the rooster begged, "and I'll give you a tooth." Accepting the rooster's tooth, Lo Kuo planted it in his garden. He gave the rooster a little water, whereupon it became Lord Thunder once again, shaking the cage apart. As sparks fly upward, so Lord Thunder ascended to heaven. Then down came a steady deluge of rain.

From the tooth in the garden there grew a long green vine, and from the vine a giant calabash ballooned, swaying upon the swirling flood. Lo Kuo climbed aboard the calabash, cut it loose, and rode the rising waters all the way to heaven, where he pounded on Lord Thunder's door. The door opened. Precipitously, the waters fell away. Plunging through space, Lo Kuo smashed his head on K'un-lun Mountain.

So ended Lo Kuo, but this mythic figure was perhaps the begetter of agriculture and therefore of civilization itself. Biologist Susumu Ohno has recently demonstrated that red jungle fowl were domesticated first in Southeast Asia, some ten thousand years ago. Melon gardening soon followed.

The giant calabash had fallen with Lo Kuo, and it also smashed. From its shattered rind a sister and a brother stepped. Lord Thunder ordered them to make children. Modestly, the brother and sister cast a double shadow on the ground. From that the Cham, Khmer, Frome, and M'ti tribes were born.

Lord Thunder is the prime regulator, a fountainhead of order and fecundity combined, who mutters off into the presexual realm. If you hear thunder rightly, your body will move lightly. You'll be able to caress the tiger and the crocodile. You shall mount the fiery phoenix if you like, or join the level "V" of the cranes' migration.

With a zip, a zoop, and one swell foop, Cook Ting chopped, sliced, slivered, and diced the dinner meats for the Queen of Banteai Srei. This went on year after year, yet Ting's cleaver stayed razorsharp, receiving never a nick or stain. Informed of the phenomenon, the Queen became curious. Calling for Ting, she had him hand over his cleaver. Avidly at first, but with mounting annoyance, she personally examined it.

"What's going on here?" said the Queen of Banteai Srei. "Why, this is just an ordinary kitchen utensil!"

"Quite so, Your Majesty."

"Well then, why doesn't it get old and scarred like other blades? What's your secret?"

"Never to sever," Ting humbly explained. "I cut nothing. Instead, I direct my blade through the emptiness which exists betwixt all things."

Upon hearing those words, the Queen of Banteai Srei fell back in her throne. She sighed deeply and then smiled, putting one finger to her lips. The nowhere-touching, everywhere-related structure of the universe stood clear to her at last.

The Grand Vizier of Banteai Srei had recently passed away, so the Queen appointed Cook Ting to replace him. Aided by Ting's counsel she became Empress of all the Khmers, and built a magical monument called Angkor Wat.

Walking between the python-railings of the causeway across the moat at Wat, I enter a narrow gate in the wall. Inside, I find a mile-square sea of grass. This comprises the core of Angkor. The breeze-teased expanse centers upon a triple temple in lotus bud form. A second python-accompanied causeway leads straight on inward to the temple, where carved stone tigers, seven-headed cobras, moneys, brahmans, and garudas, along with hundreds of dancing devatas and apsaras, movelessly gesticulate.

They're churning up inner room. To contemplate these figures is to sense the mythosphere itself expand.

Five travelers from Chunking banded together in hopes of safely crossing the Gobi desert. The first of them was a Buddhist monk, the second a desperate outlaw, the third an ink-painter, the fourth a miserly merchant, and the fifth a white-bearded sage.

On the tenth night of their journey, the companions camped outside a tall grotto in the wilderness. The full moon, rising, bathed the cavern's crystal-glittering facade in silver rays. The moonlight seemed to shatter and dissolve upon the shadowy depths beyond.

"What a great place for a hermitage," said the monk. "Or for a hideout!" the outlaw exclaimed. "It's a fine subject for my brush," said the artist. "A perfect spot to bury treasure," the miser remarked. The sage sat silent for some time. At last he spoke:

"Lovely grotto!"

Alone among the travelers, the fifth man carried home in his heart.

One sultry July noonday, with thunder rumbling at the horizon, a man named Chang lay down by the banana tree that grew in his garden. He was a bachelor, and a bit of a drunkard as well. The heavy-drooping, jade-colored leaves of the tree shaded him from the blazing sun. Bubbling out between his lips, rice-wine stained Chang's beard as he dozed. Meanwhile, an honor-guard arrived and gathered around him.

Rubbing his eyes, Chang got up. Footmen wearing liver-colored, silver-buttoned livery bowed him into a waiting rickshaw. Dozing again, he journeyed a long way. Chang entered a new country, where he was welcomed by the King and Queen.

"We sent for you, " the Queen explained, "to marry the Princess, our beautiful daughter, who is here."

"Also," the King added, "to serve in present danger, bearing this raw-silk banner around our borders, Mister Minister of War!"

Chang loved the Princess with all his heart, and on the field of battle he proved invincible. For a full year and a day, the reclusive winebibber of former times made himself useful and found himself happy. Then came a cruel twist of fate: his bride expired in childbirth. After the funeral, the Queen summoned Chang into her private chamber.

"We're soon to be destroyed by a deluge," she murmured. "Unfortunately, you're to blame!"

His dream had lasted for a few seconds only. Awakening, Chang glanced up and saw that the banana tree was leaning at a dangerous angle. Riddled by a gradual invasion of termites, its silvery trunk seemed terminally weak. Calling for an ax, Chang easily chopped down the tree. The stump resembled a hollow labyrinth, alive with scurrying ants. Peering down, wet-eyed, Chang observed his antbride's grave. The thunder sounded closer now, as huge raindrops began to fall.

The rain is Lord Thunder's daughter.

Sasaki Roshi, the egg-bald mystic of Mount Baldy, once told the following story. He had been selected, along with two other ten-year-olds, for preliminary training at a remote Zen-Buddhist monastery in northern Japan. At tea, the abbot put a test question to all three children: "How old is the Buddha?"

"Very old," the first boy replied at once, his mouth full.

"Yet ever young," the second put in.

Sasaki couldn't think of a sensible reply, so he blurted: "As old as me!"

"I like your answer best," the Abbot said, "but it's not good enough. Go sweep the veranda, then report to me in my study."

It was raining at the time. The caressing, silvery hiss of rain off the veranda roof merged with the dusty mumble of Sasaki's broom. These sounds were communicating something, but what? After finishing his work, the boy marched straight to the Abbot's private quarters. The old man sat there, still as a jar. Sasaki stood up straight and puffed out his chest.

"The Buddha is as old as the rain!"

The Abbot nodded benignly. "You've passed the first test."

Little Sasaki was right to be proud and happy. With one leap, the ten-year-old had grasped the essence of Zen. But life is an unending process of losing one's way, followed—when one is lucky— by rediscovery and ever larger horizons.

"From now on," the Abbot told him, "things will be more difficult. Here's my second question, which I want you to consider very carefully: How old is the rain?"

At that moment Sasaki commenced his life study.

* * *

My own reach toward Zen began while I was in

England writing *The Universal Myths*. Between the musty London Library, misty Ashdown Forest, and my rose-covered, family-filled Sussex cottage, I felt very nearly content. Then one night I dreamt I was a youth in old Japan.

Imagine a woodblock print by Hiroshige or Hokusai springing into life that you can touch, smell, taste, and even breathe. No longer just an image, it surrounds one totally. Something of that sort happened to me. I entered a smoother, younger existence. Breathing fresh spring air, chilly and warm at the same time, I sprang into the fragrant branches of a pine tree. The wet rough bark of the swaying pine, as I clearly recall even now, reddened the palms of my hands and stained my naked thighs.

Clambering up, up, almost to the top of the tree, I peered between its green boughs to glimpse snow-covered Mount Fuji far away.

Months later I received a postcard from a distinguished Zennist whom I'd never met. Masao Abe's card carried a reproduction of Hokusai's "Clearing Weather over Mount Fuji." It conveyed an invitation which confirmed my dream. In Kyoto the following year I practiced zazen with Abe, studied Buddhist metaphysics with Keiji Nishitani at Otani University, and cleared my head for later friendships with other masters of East-West dialogue such as Taitetsu Unno, Robert Thurman, and Eliot Deutsch.

Now what if I'd already dismissed the dream as just a sex thing, or a wish-fulfillment thing? I might have lost half my life.

The Sun and Saint Patrick

When my patron saint began his adventures, he was a pious and well-educated Welsh boy. Irish raiders captured and sold him into slavery. After some years' labor in the stony west of Eire, Patrick ran away to join an itinerant band of sorcerers.

The youth still clung to the Christian faith of his upbringing. He sorely missed Holy Mass, where he had been wont to receive the Eucharist: the transubstantiated body and blood of Christ. But the faith of Patrick's new friends centered upon the Druidic Trinity. They worshipped the Oak, the Mistletoe, and the lifegiving Sun. Their sacred rites also involved a eucharist, namely clover honey, magically transformed into the body and blood of their sun deity. Invited to partake in the Druid Mass, Patrick complied up to a point. When the holy honey was passed around, he piously compressed his lips and not a drop entered him. For this breach of ritual etiquette, he would have to pay dearly. That night, as he himself relates in his *Confession:*

> Satan assailed me violently, a thing I shall remember as long as I shall be in this body. And he fell upon me like a huge stone, and I

could not stir a limb. But whence came it into
my mind, ignorant as I am, to call upon
Helios?

The wind-whitened, earth-eaten, or water-
smoothed bones of the saints, heroes, and heroines
belonging to bygone times may rise again, but only
through the creative effort required to flesh them
out in imagination. Patrick had insulted his Druid
friends and scorned their god. Yet plainly this was
no ordinary youth; nor did he seem insensitive to
the divine. Reading between the lines of Patrick's
Confession, I suspect that the Druids subjected him
to a special version of their traditional initiation
ordeal.

Following seven years of study and apprentice-
ship, each candidate for Druid ordination was constrained to lie flat on his back with a stone slab laid
across his chest. Then, sitting at ease upon the
stone, his interlocutors leaned down to propound
abstruse riddles in the sufferer's ear. He was expected to respond knowledgeably in rhythmic, ex-
tempore verse.

Patrick was totally unprepared. His torment
went on and on, he tells us, until finally:

> I saw the sun rise in the sky, and while I
> was shouting, "Helios! Helios!" with all my
> might, suddenly the splendor of that sun fell
> on me and released me from all misery.

Along with his native Welsh and Gaelic, Patrick
spoke only Latin. Why, then, did he not cry "Sol!
Sol!," the Latin word for the sun? Why, and how,

did the Greek equivalent, "Helios," occur to him? Where could he have picked up a smattering of Greek?

The Druids were no friends to the distant, occult power of the muddy town to which ancient Rome had decayed. Nor did they themselves speak Latin. But ancient Roman and modern British historians both attest that for century after century Greek was spoken by some in Ireland. The custom apparently began with Greek trading connections during the sixth century B.C.

Every seeming miracle has a background in history and myth alike. For example, the Greek-speaking Gnostics of Egyptian Alexandria maintained that human souls are all descended from "Helios," the pre-Apollonian sun deity whom the Egyptians worshiped as "Ra." According to Firmicus Maternus, the Gnostics believed that one's spirit can reascend through the seven planetary spheres in order to reunite with Helios. Therefore, at the climax of severe initiation rites practiced by the Gnostics, the initiate was customarily crowned with a rosemary wreath and accorded a secret name: "Helios" again.

Long after Patrick's time, the medieval alchemists strove to achieve a sunlike radiance—chemically in base metals and spiritually in themselves—through an occult laboratory process which they called in Latin: "solificatio."

Comparable dynamics inform modern religious custom and belief. Consider the prophet Elijah, for example, who escaped our common fate. Instead of dying, he found himself drawn up to heaven "in a fiery chariot." The Jewish Feast of Passover in-

cludes a glass of wine set for Elijah. The prophet
lives at this very moment. He still orbits the globe
in his chariot, preparing a final mission: to lead the
Messiah down among us.

> Bring me my Bow of burning gold:
> Bring me my Arrows of desire:
> Bring me my Spear: O clouds unfold!
> Bring me my Chariot of fire!
>
> I will not cease from Mental Fight,
> Nor shall my Sword sleep in my hand
> Till we have built Jerusalem
> In England's green & pleasant Land.

So wrote the mystical engraver, painter, and poet
William Blake.

The Greek Orthodox Saint Elias also rides a fiery
chariot across the heavens. He brings thunder-
storms to fructify the rocky islands of the Aegean.
Of course the name Elias carries a strong echo of
the prophet Elijah. Then, too, it sounds very like
"Helios."

Chapels dedicated to Saint Elias crown moun-
taintops all over Greece. Most of them were originally built upon the ruins of open-air pagan altars
sacred to Phoebus Apollo, the sun god. Sunrise ser-
vices are still a feature of these places, especially at
Easter. That is, on the day of Jesus' Resurrection;
when "they found the stone rolled back from his
tomb."

At the close of his *Confession* Patrick says: "The
true sun is the Christ."

That's heresy. Saint Augustine was careful to note
that God is not the sun, but the sun's creator.

Hindu philosophers agreed in a way. Their god Vishnu, they said, is not the sun but "the Food of the Sun."

"In the beginning was the Word." Whatever begins anywhere originates there. One's own sanity and life itself may hinge upon the barest syllable. We have plausible theories concerning the creation of the sun, but nobody knows how language was born.

Or where it's leading us.

The Druids kept right after Patrick. They did everything they could to counter his increasingly successful missionary work. One day at Tara, where the High King was holding court, their High Priest abruptly demanded:

"You, now, in the presence of our King, please be so good as to justify the absurd things you say. How can your Christian deity be single and yet the same time something called a 'Holy Trinity'?"

Maintaining noble silence, Patrick stooped low. Nearsightedly, he searched the turf with his fingers for a minute or two. Then, having found what he wanted, he plucked it and stood erect once more. He showed the plant to the assembled Court. It was a common shamrock, a three-leafed clover. The very ground of Ireland had provided the needed evidence. Humbly, without a word spoken, the saint passed the supreme test of his life; turning the tide against Druid religion.

Gautama the Buddha also plucked a flower and held it up, by way of a silent sermon, to his disciples; one of whom understood what was meant.

This occurred on Raven Peak, the day of Gautama's death.

"There's nothing new under the sun," King Solomon suggested. But the Ionian sage Heraclitus added an important note: "The sun is new every day." And Saint Patrick brought something new to Ireland. Thanks to the enmity between himself and the Druids, this fresh spirit of Eire developed in tense, testy, and lovely ways. The peasants clad in forest-green, and the crimson-mantled nobles as well, were ardently Christian. Cowherds' pipes and church bells mingled with the shimmering sound of harps upon the air, crossed now and then by the clatter of polished swords. The numerous clergy spoke Latin while the equally numerous bards sang in Gaelic. Ireland was then a place of opulent simplicity, coupled with compassion for the footloose. As Bishop Cormac of Cashel wrote:

> In those days there were little cups set by wells under strict law. Hence the saying: "He suffers cups by waters." And often they were of silver, that weary travelers might drink from them . . . and kings set the cups there to test observance of the law.

And there was not one snake remaining in the whole of Ireland. This total absence of the serpent race is well attested. Naturalists cannot account for it. According to legend, Patrick simply lifted his cross against the creatures in general, bidding them begone; whereupon millions of reptiles fled the country by sea. Then, too, a host of serpent deities, meaning the red-gold dragon-forms known to

Druid practitioners, commenced their slow dissolution. Writhing, these deathless beings rode the winds away.

Time also flies, and returns. Today one still may witness dragons tear and fray like wraiths of mist upon the apple-green and blood-orange Irish sunset. Darkness comes on soon after that, and fear may follow. At least once in this life, everybody suffers paralyzing anxiety and grief. Like Saint Patrick, we also pay heavy dues to we know not what shrouded and implacable beings. Guardians of mystery they may be. Something falls upon us "like a huge stone," unavoidably crushing.

Fortunate, and very rare, is the person who can greet such horrendous episodes as aspects of spiritual struggle and opportunities for initiation.

Sleeping with Serpents

Many modern adventures of a mythic sort take place when we are ill. We wake up in hospitals, battling horrendous, lethal monsters. On the physical plane we have allies, of course. Does this keep one from feeling alone and lost? The darkest and most desperate struggles for life and renewed health are such that only oneself can undertake.

> "Know Thyself."
> "Nothing Too Much."

This key pair of precepts were inscribed on the lintels of Apollo's temple at Delphi. They're still excellent counsel for maintaining one's mental and physical equilibrium. However, Apollo's five-word advice is chillingly austere and extremely difficult to obey. Especially when it seems too late to even try.

As John Ruskin once remarked, Apollo was "lord of life, and of the three great spirits of life—Care, Memory, and Melody." This made him a severe teacher and an overwhelming lover. As so often happens, tragedy began there.

Finding Apollo's rays hard to bear, Princess Coronis of Epidaurus sought shady refuge and balm for her blisters in a mere mortal's gentler embrace. To put it bluntly, Coronis proved "unfaithful" to the solar deity—by whom she was already pregnant. For that insult to the divine order of things, Apollo's twin sister Artemis, the moon goddess, drove Coronis to destruction. The princess died in childbirth. However, her baby survived.

It was a boy. Asklepius the demigod grew up to flourish in his modest way by virtually inventing medicine. Specifically, Coronis' child adopted the hard precepts of his divine father and reshaped them to each individual case—but in gently forbearing style. Thus "Know Thyself" became a question of isolating and identifying symptoms. "Nothing Too Much" became a matter of pinpointing and moderating addictions.

Hippocrates, the renowned doctor who authored the still-operative Hippocratic Oath, lived from 460 to 377 B.C. He claimed direct descent from Asklepius, eighteen generations previous. So we are looking at a truly ancient tradition. Along with myth, art, and every other cultural artifact, medical science goes way back. This also manifests historically, often to miraculous effect.

The priests of Zeus and his proudly harsh Olympians were never quite happy with an older, humbler stream of pagan faith which centered on nature herself. So Asklepius' myth and his medical legacy both point to a concealed rift in pagan religion. Not for Asklepius were the fierce eagles, quarrelsome peacocks, spears, crested helmets, and blood sacrifices of snowy Mount Olympus. His own familiars were of the earth, earthy. Especially the harmless brown five-foot-long serpents native to sunny Epidaurus, and the loyal, wound-licking dogs of the region.

Asklepius used these, plus herbs gathered upon the mountain flanks, along with common sense—which is of course incalculably valuable—as medicinal instruments. The spring water at Epidaurus was also heartily recommended; it can be to this day. Native Greek visitors make a point of drinking from, and washing at, the water tap outside the little museum there. Me, too.

Asklepius the medical demigod was also a family man, married to Epione ("Soother"). Among their children were two heroes of the Trojan War, plus Hygeia ("Health") and Telesphoros ("Fulfillment"). People revered Asklepius himself as the original "Soter," or Savior. His final triumph was to call Hippolytus back from the dead. This compassionate interference with fate infuriated Asklepius' paternal grandfather. Zeus instantly transfixed Asklepius with a thunderbolt.

In death, the good doctor was evermore widely worshiped. He grew to be a favorite subject of classical shrine sculpture, radiating paternal nobility. Meanwhile his birthplace garnered international fame as a refuge for the sick. Epidaurus became the world's first great health clinic. In the healing business for well over a millennium, the place drew patients from all around the Mediterranean basin while spawning lesser clinics throughout the classical world.

Some sixty inscribed tablets upon which pagan patients recorded their cures have been excavated at Epidaurus. Here's one:

As I was traveling to the sanctuary, the god appeared and told me not to worry unduly. When I reached the sacred precinct he added these instructions: I was to cover my head in rainy weather, wash myself without the aid of a servant, take exercise in the gymnasterion, eat bread, cheese, celery and lettuce, drink lemon juice and milk, go for walks, and remember to perform the customary sacrificial rites. Finally, he caused me to record these matters on the present stone tablet. I leave the sanctuary cured, and grateful to the god.

Classical literature abounds in mental illness, and this too was treated at Epidaurus. How? That's a question without a clear answer. Drugs doubtless played a role. Hypnosis, also. But the chief factor seems to have been healing sleep—with serpents for cold companions.

Little is told of Morpheus, the god of sleep. That's natural, since he kept nodding off. His name identifies him with morphine, opium, and the blood-red poppy of the rock. To sleep is to dream, especially in reptile company. And it appears that dreams were as important to Asklepius' heirs as they are in modern psychoanalysis. Not that "nothing changes," rather, the mythosphere embraces past, present, and future.

Pausanius, the first travel writer, visited Epidaurus during the mid-second century A.D. Here's his account:

The sacred grove is surrounded by mountains on every side. Within the enclosure, no birth or death takes place. The image of Asklepius is of ivory and gold. The god is seated on a throne, grasping a staff in one hand, and holding the other over the head of a serpent. A dog crouches at his side. On the throne are carved in relief the deeds of Argive heroes: Bellerophon killing the Chimera, and Perseus after he has cut off the Medusa's head.

Note that neither of these lost gold or ivory bas-reliefs had to do with human combat. Instead they depicted heroes facing down creepy, disease-like entities. Chimera, first, was a fire-breather with the head of a lion, the body of a goat, and a dragon's tail. She resembled a burning fever, and she brought scorching drought until Bellerophon destroyed the monster by dropping a copper ingot down her furnace-throat.

Medusa, second, was cancerously compelling. Whoever dared to contemplate the viper-haired Gorgon head-on was instantly petrified—turned to stone. Perseus captured Medusa's reflection in a shield burnished mirror-bright. Without looking directly, he decapitated her.

The exploits of Bellerophon and Perseus plainly foreshadowed modern medical-lab victories. Pausanius continues:

> Over against the temple is the place where the suppliants of the god sleep. Near it is a white marble tholos, worth seeing. It contains a painting of Cupid minus his bow and arrows; the mischievous young deity is shown plucking a lyre.

Lust, jealousy, and lovesickness can break your heart. The pagan poets regarded heartbreak far more seriously than we do today. In the classical view this was a form of madness. Cupid, the boy-god of love, was an archer who never went weaponless. His arrows made men and women crazy, obsessed with greedy passion for each other's bodies and souls. However, the lost Cupid fresco in the tholos at Epidaurus presented a totally different concept. There the god of love was shown at peace, playing a lyre. In this mural Cupid was playful, perhaps, but not mischievous.

Whatever discord or despair we bring to our own amorous relationships, the tholos fresco implied, love itself is a matter of creative harmony. Striking the right chords, as it were. Here's Pausanius again:

> The other fresco in the tholos depicts Silenus imbibing from a crystal goblet. You can see not only the transparent goblet with the wine in it, but also a woman's face gleaming through the glass.

Alcoholism has come to be regarded as an incurable disease which goes with a lonely, self-despising mindset. The pagan poets took a less sympathetic view. Silenus, the donkey-riding Greek god of drunkenness, was traditionally depicted as paunchy, pie-eyed, and out of it; a contemptible figure of fun. He chased after women; they never came to him. But at Epidaurus this tradition was deliberately reversed. Silenus was shown elegantly imbibing from a crystal goblet, through which a woman's face appeared.

If the first fresco in the tholos accorded creative dignity to Cupid, this one, standing opposite, accorded visionary warmth to Silenus. In both cases the message was the same. Addiction to love, or wine for example, can make one ill. But gods are gods. It's no use blaming them for what we do.

Live in the moment, we're told. "Gather ye rosebuds while ye may." Enjoy to the full. But on the other hand, to totally lose oneself in the moment is to forget both self and it. The whole thing winks into nothingness, and who wants that? If I gobble my good moments, then they're gone. After "having sex," they say, everyone is sad. Naturally. But after making love in the genuine sense, sexually or otherwise, no one is unhappy.

Gratitude is the sunshine of inner existence. Just now I'm enjoying a special memory of Epidaurus. During the final miraculous moonburst of her career, Maria Callas sang there in the opera *Norma*. Her voice was going, but that night she didn't care. Nor did I, nor anyone else there. The occasion itself triumphed, obliterating all fear.

The amphitheater at Epidaurus dates from the fourth century B.C. Designed by Polyclitus, it's an architectural masterpiece of the first order. Although it can hold fifteen thousand people, the amphitheater seems intimate, and its bell-clear acoustics augment that impression. The marble structure appears to rest easy, like a pure half-cupful of air, between earth and sky. On the balmy night that *Norma* was performed a full moon shone, well suiting the Druidic subject. At one point a gleaming space satellite slowly passed overhead. The serendipitous synchronicity of this roused a prolonged "Ahhh"—a lovely sound—from the assembled throng. Modern science, ancient legend, a classic ambiance, a brave performance, and immortal music, all coalesced. That was a moment to remember.

I'm for the greatest and most widely sparkling present moment possible. Let it have a darkly vivid, immediate center, experienced up-close, with luminous flower-petal ripples expanding out upon the past and future. In other words let it be Dionysian at the intimate core and Apollonian in its radiant scope. And may such moments return to lighten one's less happy days; times of sickness, for example.

John de Conquer

Twenty-four pears hung on a tree, twelve of them high and twelve low. Twelve kings came riding by. Each took one. How many were left?

None? If each of the twelve kings had taken a pair for himself, yes. But in fact the kings were thinking only of their own appearances. Not one so much as paused to peer at the pears on the tree. They rode on by.

Each took one. Nobody else did. Twenty-three remained.

As with the pears on the tree, so it is with challenge and adventure in the mythosphere. There's always more than one expects.

John de Conquer was a deep-sea fisherman. On his twenty-first birthday, John caught no less than seven big tunafish. When he returned to land, he saw a pair of lions making love on the beach. That was something new to him. John put his tunafish in a sack, slung it across his back, and went to consult the Witch Woman of the Gullah.

"These are for you," he said. "Please help me to find my heart's desire."

The Witch Woman looked at him: "What would that be, my son?"

"I don't know!"

"All right, in that case I can help."

Between John de Conquer's knees a giant crow appeared. John found himself sitting high up astride the neck of the crow, who croaked: "Where to?"

"I don't know."

"In that case, I can help." And away flew the crow, westward over the Atlantic Ocean, with John riding him. After three hundred miles of steady flying the crow spoke again.

"I'm tired and hungry, my son, but there's no solid ground for us to land upon."

"Here's food for you!" John cried. He tossed up a tuna, which the crow caught in its beak and swallowed whole.

After they'd flown another three hundred miles the crow repeated his plaint, and again John de Conquer fed him. This went on until all seven tunafish were gone. Then the crow began to weaken and to shrink in size, skimming lower and lower through the clouds. Luckily they were over land once more. They came down in a bluegrass field. As John dismounted, the crow disappeared. Instead, there stood the loveliest person John had ever seen. She was an onyx-black girl, aged sixteen or so, with long curly hair and a warm smile of welcome. "Why are you here?" she asked.

"This time," John said, "I know the answer. I've come to marry you!"

"That won't be so easy," said the girl, and tears rolled down her cheeks as she spoke. "For I'm the Devil's daughter, and here's my father now!"

The Devil was a big old creature, pale as a shark in color, with icy blue eyes. He wore a white fedora and carried a fly whisk. "I heard you talking," said the Devil, "and I'm a reasonable man. So if you'll do three little jobs for me, then you can have my daughter."

"What's the first job?"

"Look at my hundred-acre forest over there. Clear all those trees away for me tomorrow. If you're not finished by sundown, I'll tear off your arms and legs."

By noon the next day, John de Conquer was in despair. He'd felled only thirty trees when the Devil's daughter appeared. "Give me that ax," she said. "I'll speak to it." Putting the blade to her cheek, she whispered a few words, whereupon the ax flew off to demolish and clear the whole forest in half an hour's time.

At sunset the Devil came along. "What's the next job?" John said.

"Tomorrow, plow the whole hundred acres for me. If that isn't done before the sun goes down again, I'll boil you in oil."

John got up good and early the next day. By noon, however, he had plowed only thirty furrows across the field. Then, as before, the Devil's daughter appeared. "Let me speak to your plow," she said. At her bidding the plow raced off through the turf, turning it this way and that, until the whole field lay properly furrowed.

The Devil showed himself just as the sun was going down. "You've done good," he said to John de Conquer. "I hate you for that."

"What's my final job?"

"For a great magician such as you, the last task should be easy. In the morning, plant my field with corn. Make it grow right away. In the afternoon, reap the harvest for me. If my corn's not in the barn by sunset tomorrow, I'll bury you alive."

That night, the Devil's daughter came to John. "Father aims to kill you no matter what," she told him. "Let's get out of here!" Holding hands, they ran away across the plantation, through the woods and on over high, smoky hills by moonlight. Fortunately John de Conquer was a strong, speedy man. By dawn the Devil's daughter had begun to tire, so he picked her up and carried her across one shoulder. Looking back, just as the sun came up, she glimpsed her father hastening after them.

His big old boots were steaming, and as he clumped along the Devil spoke. "Step lively, boots! Jump it! Make each step a mile long!"

The Devil's daughter drew from her hair a small tortoiseshell comb. Holding this to her lips, she murmured a few urgent words. Then she let the comb drop to the ground. Instantly a blackberry bush sprang up, speedily spreading out in all directions. The bush grew and grew until it measured about a mile high and twice as thick. The Devil made a great jump to get over the blackberry bush. He fell right in the midst of it.

Most scholars would relegate this story to a realm which they consider inferior. Proper myth, they might explain, deals with grander themes in relatively adult and solemn style.

But folktale and fairytale also belong to the mythosphere. Their tradition is even more ancient than Homer or the Bible, for example, and their influence is far greater than generally realized. Such stories constitute our first introduction to the fabulous. They gently lead children to recognize that there is a war on earth between good and evil. Also that terrible dangers abound—threats which we can overcome. Thus fairytales and folktales reinforce the child's inborn wonder, reverence, and courage. And, as I have found, they refresh those same qualities in adulthood.

One further point. Legends such as John de Conquer's help to cushion a youngster's free-fall into what we regard as the "real world," with all its bruisingly material and rational constraints. They instill confidence, which will help one to survive later crises of faith. So parents and others who pass this kind of myth on to children—not just in book form but orally—perform invaluable service.

P'an-Hu

Beauty and the Beast often start their relationship in a stormy way. Either because the world tries to separate them or because each becomes a sore trial to the other. Yet, whether they be together or apart, gradually the two grow lovingly aware of each other's problems and qualities. Finally winning out against enormous odds, they come to share one and the same existence. They experience beautiful force and tender courage in the same breath—which is happiness.

This legend is universal, naturally, since it concerns everybody. The earliest version of the myth that I have found appears in a very ancient Confucian text called *Hou Han Shu*, or "Annals of the Later Han." Here it is:

Huffing and puffing in a fit of fatherly fury, the Han Emperor Kao-hsin banished a courtier named Wu for lascivious behavior. Specifically, for having presumed to eye the Emperor's own daughter in a lovesick manner. The Princess had been seen to blush. Wu's affront to her virgin sensibility outraged the entire Court.

Holing up, disgraced, amid the Mountains of the West, Wu gathered a raggle-taggle band of army deserters around himself. Wu's Raiders proceeded to terrorize the foothill provinces, almost at will. There seemed no way to put an end to these lightning depredations. The moment that Han troops appeared, the bandits vanished in among the mist-hung cliffs. This situation disturbed the Emperor's rest, and it was much discussed. Finally Kao-hsin proclaimed that any hero brave and wily enough to destroy Wu—and bring his head to Court—would be rewarded with a fiefdom of ten thousand families, plus the Princess' hand in marriage.

Soon afterward, a very large, multicolored mastiff appeared at the palace gate. Wu's head hung by the hair from between the beast's slavering jaws. Overjoyed, the Emperor had the head transferred to a flagpole atop a high porcelain pagoda. There Wu's wild visage dangled, danced, and spun about until the carrion ravens of the capital had plucked it clean.

Kao-hsin meanwhile ordered that the multicolored mastiff receive every honor appropriate to its canine station.

"Not good enough," the Princess sighed: "You must keep your royal promise and marry me off to this bloodthirsty animal, whom I shall call P'an-hu."

The wedding ceremony was performed purely as a matter of protocol, or so the Court assumed. That night, however, the Princess rode away on P'an-hu's back. The Emperor sent his own bodyguard in pursuit. Encountering heavy storms, they lost the animal's track. Kao-hsin believed his daughter dead: eaten, perhaps. He commanded that twelve months of mourning—"The Year of the Dog"—be observed throughout his empire.

A generation passed, the Emperor fell ill, and then one day the Princess returned to embrace her dying father.

"P'an-hu, my husband, has passed on," she said. "However, our twelve sons and daughters live and prosper beyond the Mountains of the West. By way of tribute to yourself, their grandfather, whose distant rule they dimly acknowledge, the children sent along this bundle of twisted bark garments, together with this sack of varicolored licorice."

Having admired and put away the odd garments, the Emperor tried the licorice candy. He loved the stuff. It restored not only his health but also his lost youth. The newly vigorous Kao-Hsin begged his daughter to tell about P'an-Hu.

"He wasn't really a dog, was he?"

"Sometimes," the Princess replied. "Then again, he'd be a headless man."

"How dreadful!"

"Not at all. What happened was this. General Wu loved me, as you're aware. I loved him too, which you didn't know. Secretly we picked a ton of rice, as the peasants say, before you shooed my winsome Wu away."

"Oh, my dear!"

"You're quite right to be sorry. Our forced separation proved unutterably painful and cruel, not only for me but for Wu too. Then came your generous offer concerning Wu's head. When the proclamation was published I sent a spirit-body to the Mountains of the West."

"Could you do that?"

"Yes, though I paid a price."

"I noticed at the time that you were looking thin."

"After three nights of moonlit wandering, my spirit-body managed to locate Wu. In the crystal cavern below Kun-l'un, a fleshless connection occurred. It wasn't bad! Afterward, with my spirit-body's assistance, Wu took the form of a canine deity. Namely, the primordial P'an-hu."

"Unbelievable!"

"Fortunately for Wu's plan, this divine animal has no place in the pantheon of Han. Many centuries ago it was dropped from civilized discourse. Hence the bark—"

"Bark?"

"Things do get complicated. They worked out well, however."

This legend concludes with the rejuvenated Emperor enthusiastically applauding his daughter. "One Han clapping," as it were.

Some scholars may argue that my oriental *Beauty and The Beast*, like "John de Conquer," is sheer entertainment of a minor sort. But its real subject is tremendously important. Thomas Jefferson spelled out humanity's inalienable right to "the Pursuit of Happiness." And, as Robert Louis Stevenson remarked, "There is no duty that we so much underrate as the duty of being happy."

The Guide of Souls

Plato affirmed that if we believe the Myth of Er we shall safely cross the River of Forgetfulness. It's assumed that the philosopher was talking about death, but the "River of Forgetfulness" makes a telling image for life itself, as generally lived. Here's the story, recorded by Plato himself:

A man named Er, the son of Armenius, was slain in battle. After twelve days and nights he returned to life, bringing a true account from beyond the grave. The dead, Er reported, are all destined to live again. They draw lots. Then each in turn is permitted to choose a new existence from among many, many possibilities.

Thus the embittered soul of Ajax—that bluff, unbeatable warrior whom Odysseus had outfoxed—chose to become a lion in his next incarnation; ranging far from the haunts of treacherous mankind. And Agamemnon, who had returned in triumph from Troy only to be murdered by his wife Clytemnestra, sought similar release. Eagerly Agamemnon leaped to select an eagle-life. The Mycenian monarch hoped that by soaring afar upon the upper air he might finally clear himself of the family curse.

And it fell out that the soul of Odysseus drew the last lot of all, and came to make its choice, and, from memory of its former toils having flung away ambition, went about for a long time in quest of the life of an ordinary citizen who minds his own business. He found this lying in a corner, disregarded by the others . . . and chose it gladly.

Plato may have been correct. However, Philostratus of Alexandria maintained that Odysseus was not modest at all. Following his death the "man of many devices" undertook a spirit-quest, Philostratus tells us, for eternal renown. After some centuries, he found Homer. The poet bowed his blind head to listen and remember as the old captain's words fell harsh and slow, dictating *The Odyssey.*

Behind Odysseus stands a saucy sorceress. Her name, Circe, refers to the seasonal cycle with its equinoxes and solstices, as well as the encircling horizon seen from a ship at sea. Circe's father was Helios, the saucer-faced sun deity who is so luminous that he seems black to look upon. Her mother was Irish, the Amazon Queen Cessair. Her home was Aeaea, a floating island which bobbed along and around the furthest fringes of the time stream. The name Aeaea itself sounds like a distant cry. Once, very long ago, lost on his way home to Ithaca, Odysseus landed there. Cautiously, the captain sent a few crewmen inland to explore.

Black in a blazing white apron, Circe crossed the sailors' path and invited them to enter her kitchen. Once they were comfortable she rang a little bell, whereupon a feast appeared. The sailors fell to it greedily, with Circe looking on. Again she rang her bell. With sighs of satisfaction the crewmen glanced up over their round cups and platters. Lithe, luxurious, robed in darkness and light, Circe danced from right to left. Her whispering steps upon the sanded floor conspired with the sinuous motions of her arms to weave an invisible skein around the whole assembly. Softly she waved a fragrant sprig of tamarisk over each sailor. Grunting, they slipped and fell down one by one from the benches, transformed into swine.

When Odysseus himself came shambling bearishly along in search of his men, he was armed with a magic herb even more powerful than Circe's tamarisk. "Mole," this medicine was called. He had received it, just a few minutes previously, from Hermes, the guide of souls.

Thanks to mole, Circe fell in love with Odysseus on sight. For his sake she turned the swine back into sailors again. But they regretted that. Circe's sties were preferable, all agreed, to coming death by water. The sorceress meanwhile drew Odysseus to her five-sided bed. Tongue-smooth, shadow-soft, Circe's embrace restored his sea-shrunken strength fivefold. Concerning this episode, little more is said. But Odysseus and his crew lingered on Aeaea until she had borne him three sons: Agrius, Latinus, and Telegonus.

And finally, Circe confided to her lover the secret of consorting with the dead.

Plato's myth of Er came true at last in Odysseus' case. That wayworn wanderer did eventually claim "the life of an ordinary citizen who minds his own business." Twist the millennial tumblers of time, and once again Odysseus appears. But now he's a printed being; his bones are the spines of books. In fact he's suffered a complete sea change, and change of name: to Leopold Bloom. No longer a heroic adventurer under sail, he stands reduced to a Dublin ad salesman—mind the puns—in James Joyce's novel *Ulysses.*

A lapidary master of literary legerdemain, Joyce made words coruscate and twist about like the dragon-tailed initials which ornament *The Book of Kells.* He created Leopold Bloom as a thoughtful but ordinary, garden-variety sort of man. But Bloom dimly dreamed of performing high deeds indeed, such as shooting "self-compelled, to the extreme limit of his cometary orbit, beyond the fixed stars and the variable suns."

Thought-processes are volatile; Bloom's were deliciously so. Abruptly descending from far-out space, he entertained himself with ashen fantasies of death: "Is his nose pointed is his jaw sinking are the soles of his feet yellow. Pull the pillow away and finish it off on the floor since he's doomed."

Bloom was attending a friend's funeral at that point. Meanwhile his wife Molly chose to entertain at home. Molly was wide-thighed, with a melony belly, azure-veined breasts that bobbled when she laughed, and warmly promiscuous habits. Very different, in short, from Odysseus' faithful spouse. No Penelope, she. Here's Molly musing on the afternoon:

> . . . this old bed too jingling like the dickens
> I suppose they could hear us away over to the

> other side of the park till I suggested to put
> the quilt on the floor with the pillow under
> my bottom. . . .

Circe-like, Molly Bloom made pigs of certain
guests. Then, too, she made a sadder, wiser man of
her domestic adventurer: Bloom himself. And as
her name implies, Molly also incorporated a most
mysterious magic herb in her makeup:

"Mole." It's got a delicate white blossom and a
deep black root. Very difficult to locate, it's almost
impossible to grasp.

One sunny day in 1787, Johann Wolfgang von
Goethe sat quietly on a bench in the Botanical Garden at Palermo, Sicily. The teary-eyed author of
The Sorrows of Young Werther had reached the age
of thirty-eight and come to the end of his romantic
tether. He was on a two-year journey down from
Germany in search of inspiration. The cool, clean-
contoured clarity of the remaining classical sculpture and architecture that he encountered in Italy
had already done much to persuade Goethe that
intellect itself possesses concreteness. Like a culti-
vated mind, the deep-colored, sharp-shadowed
glow of Palermo's Botanical Garden seemed to confirm that happy impression.

Goethe had faith in the existence of actual ideas.
That is, things of the mind which are not merely
symbolic and not confined to combinations of
words or numbers. Actual ideas, he decided, are
timeless. Moreover, they sometimes engage the
imagination so intently that one can witness them
and even interact with them in a physical sense.

Just now, Goethe was pondering a play that he planned to write about Odysseus. He began turning over in his mind a scene in which Odysseus would receive from Hermes' hand the sacred and mysterious herb by which to seduce Circe. It occurred to him that "mole," the magic herb in question, was a good example of an actual idea. At that very moment, Hermes the pagan guide of souls approached the poet himself. The god struck open Goethe's interior vision and pointed to a greenly unfolding form.

The poet named this *Urpflanze,* which translates as urplant or primordial vegetable. Gratefully, Goethe abandoned all thought of writing about Odysseus. Instead, he composed a seminal essay concerning biological metamorphoses. They stem, he argued, from the archetype that drives plant life. In other words, from a neo-Platonic "Idea."

Goethe's description of the *Urpflanze* was couched in soberly scientific language. However, it owed much to the poet's long and loving acquaintance with alchemical lore. The Philosopher's Stone was a terribly elusive esoteric goal of alchemy—far more important than creating gold. The Stone was thought to contain a "female" aspect symbolized by the lily. In alchemical texts this magical flower was called "Lili," "Lilie," and "Lilly." Paracelsus spoke of it:

> The matter of the Tincture is a very great pearl and a most precious treasure, and the noblest thing next to the manifestation of the Most High. This is the Lili of Alchemy and of Medicine.

Another alchemist whom Goethe had perused with special interest was George Starkey. In convincingly ecstatic terms Starkey proclaimed:

> Then shall thy Elements perfectly accord, and one color shall cover thy newly-married Soul and Body, and that will be like to the most pure Lilly, or sublimed salt, sparkling like to a new-slipped Sword in the Sunbeams.

Looking at an actual lily, I might well see it as an exquisitely delicate, helpless, ephemerally beautiful creature, doomed to wither and die. If so, I've failed to observe it *"mit den Augen des Geistes,"* as Goethe wrote. That is, with the eyes of the spirit. Wistfully bearing witness to one passing moment of an individual flower's existence on a one-way time-line is insufficient.

To assess the lily rightly, I would have to watch its entire time-span in my imagination. Then and only then would I witness the lily blossom's cool blaze as the apogee of a cyclical life-process which arcs from seed to seed. Only by focusing the roundness of my mind's eye upon the whole life-cycle of an individual flower can I begin to sense its mythic power and glory.

Doesn't something of the same sort apply to humans? Not only will we die, but we've been born, and we have grown, and there is more. Whether on earth, or sea, or in our hearts alone, each one of us adventures far. We wrestle long and hard, both with others and with ourselves. We suffer, all of us, together or apart. We may even seize paradise, once or twice, by the fragrant locks of desire.

"All things pass by us, or we pass by them." So wrote the ancient Greek poet Menander. Technically correct and coldly clear, Menander's comment left out something—namely Hermes, the guide of souls. I'll quote from the Homeric Hymn concerning him:

> When the purpose of great Zeus was fulfilled, and Maia's tenth moon was fixed in heaven, she bore a son of many shifts, blandly cunning, a robber, a cattle-driver, a bringer of dreams, a watcher by night, a thief at the gates, who was soon to show forth wonderful deeds among the deathless gods. Born with the dawn, at midday he played upon the lyre, and in the evening he stole the cattle of far-shooting Apollo.

This enigmatically smiling deity heralds with one hand while stealing with the other. The clue to his true nature lies there.

Hermes is on our side. Always has been. He brings freedom for becoming. He nurtures experience of life. Significant experience is a most potent herb. And the guide of souls is more than a god. He demands no worship, only recognition as an actual idea.

The idea of real time.

PART TWO

The Power
of Images

Introduction

Intolerance is the father of illusion and evil deeds. Tolerance is not its opposite; tolerance is neutral. The opposite of intolerance is creative imagination, sympathetically exercised in the service of ever-illusive truth. The people whom I most trust and admire take that path. Scholars, scientists, priests, and philosophers have helped guide me through the mythosphere. A fiery legion of artists and writers flung wide the gates and beckoned my near-sighted soul to go deeper.

Like transparent treasure afloat upon the air, deathless works of art embellish and exercise human imagination. They help us to partake in the mythosphere. That's the first and foremost power of art at its height.

The second power is relatively obvious, but awesome all the same. Great art concretizes and preserves. It lends earthly, material, and time-bound existence to matters which are essentially spiritual and timeless.

Through the creative play of one's own imagination—when it's sparked by intellectual curiosity and nourished by heartfelt concern—truth manifests. Or does she? This question drives philosophers to distraction. It raises hell with religion, as well.

Saint Dionysius the Areopagite, and Marsilio Ficino after him, maintained that we never see truth running naked beside us, yet there she is at all times. To make her presence felt, she dons rainbow garments. Only then, from a corner of the eye, may one glimpse the lady dimly dancing, glancing curiously by.

The third and final power of art is to assist in this process. A few masterpieces enable truth to reveal something of herself; they make visible the invisible. But not in public. This seeming miracle seldom occurs in private, either, and then only as a momentary one-on-one shock of recognition between you and the work of art in question. Still, it does happen. Anyone who peruses Shakespeare, Goethe, or Dostoevsky, with full and sympathetic attention, can testify to this. So can anyone who looks long and lovingly at certain paintings, shrines, and statuary.

Early in the eighth century of our era, the Byzantine Emperor Leo III raised his scepter and decreed that all holy images are inherently unholy. They must be destroyed, he declared, thus unleashing civil war throughout Christendom. This conflict persisted intermittently until the mid-ninth century, with "iconoclasts" like Leo on one side, and "iconodules" such as the Empress Irene on the other.

Jewish religion stood opposed to "pagan idolatry" and the making of "graven images." Why should Christian religion allow them? In the long run, reasoned the iconoclasts, spiritual things are all that matter. Spirit has no visible form. Therefore to picture things of the spirit is misleading, evil, and blasphemous.

Although new on the scene, iconoclasm had long roots. Vedantic philosophy maintained that corporeal experience is nothing but a veil of illusions. Plato described human perceptions as mere shadows on the wall of a cave. Only the ideal is real in any lasting sense, he explained. Saint Paul transposed the Platonic perspective to history. "The present form of this world," he warned, "is passing away." Saint Ignatius of Antioch carried the iconoclastic line of thought to a dreadfully blinkered conclusion: "Nothing that is visible is good."

Yet, as far back as anyone could remember, people had witnessed spiritual happenings and also represented spirit in material form. Moses acknowledged Jehovah's presence in a burning bush, for example, and Christian hermits kept crosses in their caverns. An Arab Christian icon-painter, Saint John Damascene of Syria, presented the iconodules' case in a famous treatise, as follows:

> The Apostles saw Christ bodily, his sufferings and his miracles, and they heard his words. We desire also to see, and to hear, in order to be happy. . . . We are double beings with a body and a soul, and our soul is not naked but rather surrounded as with a cloak. It is impossible for us to have access to the spiritual without the corporeal. While listening to audible words we hear with our corporeal ears and thus grasp spiritual things. In the same way,

it is through corporeal seeing that we arrive at spiritual insight.

Nothing is more irritating, to a fanatic, than common sense. And nothing is more dangerous than a ruler convinced of his own righteousness. Enraged by John's treatise, the Emperor Leo played a very dirty trick. He had a letter forged in Saint John's handwriting. Addressed to himself as emperor of Byzantium, the letter urged that he invade Syria. Leo forwarded this false document to the Syrian Caliph with a friendly note:

"Apparently you have a Christian traitor at Court."

The caliph sent for John. "The hand that wrote this letter," he fumed, "will be removed for my dogs to chew upon. How do you like that?"

With a single swift scimitar-swipe the caliph's executioner cut off John's right hand, which fell fluttering to the carpet. John quickly bent down to retrieve it in his left hand and clap it back upon his wrist again. Earnestly proclaiming his innocence, he prayed to the Virgin Mary for vindication.

Legend relates that the severed parts miraculously grew together once more. The Damascene's writing and painting hand proved to be as good as new, with its prodigious skills intact as well.

Afterward, by way of celebration, Saint John painted an icon of the Virgin showing three hands: her own, together with his hand which she had saved. Thus a new icon tradition, that of the three-handed Virgin, was born. It came to be regarded allegorically. The Mother of God has her own hands plus a third which she extends to help each and every suppliant in time of need.

Truth does the same, but only when her hand is ardently sought.

Indian summer had come to Manhattan. I was sitting on a bench down by the Sailboat Pond in Central Park. The children's bright-colored clothes, the white sails of the model boats, the occasional black-and-white of a governess' uniform, the purplish glitter of the wind-rippled water, the scruffy brown hillside, the great trees beginning to be touched with cadmium-yellow and lipstick-red, and finally the cool stone gleam of Fifth Avenue apartment houses forming a cliff against the opal sky, dimly impressed themselves upon my consciousness.

At the same time I was recalling Sassetta's *Journey of the Magi,* a small Siennese panel which dates from the early fifteenth century. I'd spent the morning at the Metropolitan Museum, just a block north of my park bench, studying Sassetta's picture.

The painting's pure, chill colors ring as clear as children singing a carol. Six geese arrow through the still dark upper air. Winter dawn rises behind the pink walls of Jerusalem on the horizon. The hilly ground is bare. The trees are bare. Horses, dogs, baggage-masters, pageboys, knights, courtiers in quilted tunics, a falconer, a monkey on a palanquin, a jester, and three richly robed riders with gold-encircled heads descend a stony track. They're following a strange thing, a spiky gold-leaved abstraction which floats before them a few

feet off the ground. Two magpies, birds of immor-
tality, accompany this apparition, or guiding star,
which leads the Magi on toward Bethlehem.

Like a mist of colored droplets through which I
still discerned the actual Central Park scene, Sassetta's *Journey of the Magi* glistened in my mind's
eye. Jerusalem's walls cast a veiling shimmer across
Fifth Avenue's apartment towers, and the Star of
Bethlehem hung in a yellowing grove of trees off
to the right of where I sat. It resembled a sea urchin,
or rather, an air urchin, of dazzling light. I squinted
at the star, trying to make out its details amid the
leaves.

Instead, a totally different picture emerged. A
South Sea Garden of Eden bloomed in my mind's
eye.

A carved wooden idol darkly brooded over the
scene. The idol was attended, in a desultory way,
by several savages whose goldenly glowing bodies
appeared composed of earth well mixed with honey
and warm breath. Ranging from old age all the way
down to infancy, they appeared tender together, yet
each one alone at the same time—comforting yet
comfortless figures in a dream of departed friends.

What happened to the Sassetta? Why had this
darker, warmer, and more imperative picture
rushed up from within me? Why did this imbue
my Central Park reverie, steeping and staining the
whole thing? Near the center, a radiant youth stood
reaching high over his head to pluck down something from above. An apple, or a crystal, or a star?
For a second or two I didn't know.

The actual painting had roughly the same propor-
tions as the Sassetta, but it was thirty or forty times

larger. Paul Gauguin painted this on burlap in 1898. The Boston Museum of Fine Arts has it.

In youth I'd worshiped Gauguin's masterpiece. As for the youth in the painting, he does in fact reach up to pluck some sort of fruit from the very top of the image. His feet are firmly planted upon island ground. His toes nearly touch the picture's bottom rim. He's a living column which bisects the composition, and a South Sea Adam beneath the Tree of Life.

Gauguin did not find his inspiration in Tahiti. Rather, it arose volcanically from undersea mountains of dream. But the islanders amongst whom the artist made his final home were like cousins to him—and to us. There's a child in every man and woman, a hidden self who understands the poetry of life but not the prose.

"Poetry in a painter is something special; it's neither illustration nor a formal transcription." So wrote Gauguin. He was perhaps the first artist to be explicit about that. "In painting as in music," Gauguin explained, "one must search for suggestion rather than description. People accuse me of being incomprehensible only because they keep looking for an explicative side to my pictures, which is not there."

After completing his masterpiece and shipping it off to France with some other pieces for exhibition, Gauguin attempted suicide by poison. Syphilis was slowly killing him; he wished to accelerate the process. Unluckily he overdosed himself, vomited the whole business up, and lived on in Tahiti in terrible pain. Then came a packet of unfavorable reviews from Paris. André Fontainas complained in his review that the title which Gauguin had chosen for his big picture was "too literary." The artist sent Fontainas a letter, which read in part:

> I paint and dream at the same time, with no tangible allegory in mind—perhaps due to a lack of literary education. Awakening with my work finished, I ask myself these questions—
> Where do we come from? What are we? Where are we going?

Those three basic questions were Gauguin's title for his masterpiece. Nobody on earth can answer them. At least not for anyone else. And who can explain, let alone justify, the intense suffering on every hand? Syphilis, for example, decimated both Tahiti and the Latin Quarter of Paris in Gauguin's time. Like AIDS today, it was a ubiquitous presence which induced both pity and terror.

Art does not confer freedom from pity and terror. In fact they're part of it. Nor does art offer knowledge of where one is going. The Three Wise Men or Magi followed their Star in conscious ignorance of where it might lead. And that was how Gauguin followed his dream. As Saint Gregory of Nyassa long ago explained:

> Its object of desire being infinite, art's movement will never cease to be carried perpetually forward, for it will never discover a limit to what it seeks.

"Mark this horror, and this, and this," Fritz Eichenberg's wormily grooving burin suggests.

"Have a good cry; it could be you." Then, with a rueful smile, this woodcut illustrator slips in something for us to laugh about. Born German-Jewish in the fateful year 1900, my late friend lived through most of the century. That gave him a lot to brood over and blast as best he could. Finding refuge in America, Eichenberg became a Quaker as well as an ally of the Catholic socialist Dorothy Day. ("Don't call me a saint," said Dorothy Day. "I refuse to be dismissed so easily.")

Millions of us carry Eichenberg's illustrations around, imbedded in our psyches. They recall passages from Erasmus, Shakespeare, Swift, Poe, the Brontë sisters, Kipling, Pushkin, Turgenyev, Tolstoy, Dostoevsky, and many more. One of Eichenberg's most private and powerful sketches shows Dostoevsky hunched over a desk, hollow-eyed with painful visions as he writes. Meanwhile at the author's back a light-filled figure stands waiting. This second figure is radiantly calm and straight, shining with profound goodwill. The hard-laboring author doesn't look back to see this sustaining presence, yet perhaps he may feel it. Who or what stands behind Dostoevsky the writer? Eichenberg's drawing makes that crystal clear. It's a second Dostoevsky: the true spirit of the man himself.

When God created Adam, he used a handful of dust for the purpose. Was it plain ordinary dust? Yes, but from all over the world. Dostoevsky and Eichenberg have both returned, as it were, to dust. But their spirit-doubles lived—and yet live—in a timeless place. Saint John the Divine described this best in his Revelation:

There came unto me one of the seven angels which had one of the seven vials filled with the seven last plagues. . . . He carried me away in spirit to a lofty mountain and showed me that great city, the holy Jerusalem. . . . And he that talked with me had a golden reed to measure the city. . . . And he measured the wall thereof one hundred and forty and four cubits according to the measure of man; that is, of the angel. And the building of the wall of it was of jasper: and the city was pure gold, like unto clear glass. . . . And I saw no temple therein: for the Lord God Almighty and the Lamb are the temple of it. . . . And the nations of them which are saved shall walk in the light of it: and the kings of the earth do bring their glory and honor into it. And the gates of it shall not be shut at all. . . .

The Bible, the Koran, and the vastitude of the Talmud contain more than enough cornerstones for the building of a New Jerusalem; if ever our common dust agrees.

Gray and Black

"I never saw anything so impudent on the walls of any exhibition, in any country, as last year in London." So wrote the revered critic John Ruskin. "It was a daub professing to be a 'Harmony in Pink and White' (or some such nonsense); absolute rubbish, and which had taken about a quarter of an hour to scrawl, or daub—it had no pretense to be called painting."

James McNeill Whistler, the artist whom Ruskin had so rudely blindsided, responded in kind:

> "Art, that for ages has hewn its own history in marble, and written its own comments on canvas, shall it suddenly stand still, and stammer, and wait for wisdom from the passer-by? For guidance from the hand that holds neither brush nor chisel?

"Aestheticism" was Whistler's wispy war banner, which he waved with high, swishing style. The Buddhist ideal of peaceful detachment appealed to Whistler, yet he himself was loftily contentious and preeningly proud. The artist professed delight "that we can't see ourselves as others see us. . . . I know in my case I should grow intolerably conceited."

Such creative lights of Victorian London as George Meredith, Algernon Charles Swinburne, Ellen Terry, Dante Gabriel Rossetti, Walter Sickert—and Oscar Wilde for awhile—believed in him. "Art never expresses anything but itself," Wilde had written. But in fact the painter and his friends were few against many. The public was by no means ready for what Whistler had to offer. So he was unwise to sue Ruskin for slander.

Sneeringly "rewarded" with a single farthing in damages, he found himself laughed out of court. Still adamantly unappreciated by the public, Whistler died in 1903. How differently we look upon his work today!

America is short on mother-figures. Pocohontas and Betsy Ross pale before our Founding Fathers in general. We do have the Statue of Liberty, but that's hardly a sufficient counterpoise for Mount Rushmore, the Washington Monument, and the Lincoln Memorial. Our North American heritage contains a ton of Dads, in other words, but precious little that's maternal. That may be why we tend to revere "Whistler's Mother."

The picture hangs in Paris and is known to most Americans only through reproduction, yet this painting has become a veritable icon in our consciousness.

The impulse at work dates from way, way back. Isis nurtured, guided, and guarded the ancient Egyptians. Artemis was a virgin mother to the Lydians of Asia Minor, as Athena was to the Greeks. The Madonnas painted by Cimabue, Giotto, Giovanni Bellini, Leonardo, Raphael, and Titian, among others, brought more than comfort and beauty to Renaissance Italy. They manifested a universal ideal.

"I do not choose to be born at Lowell, Massachusetts!" Whistler complained. Nonetheless, a certain arid, New England secularity was built into the artist. His masterpiece conveys Whistler's reticent Yankee background rather than his foreground life as a diner-out of fulminating wit and a London dandy in lemon spats. *Arrangement in Gray and Black* was Whistler's own title for the canvas.

By way of a subtitle he remarked off-handedly that, "One does like to make one's Mummy just as nice as possible." Clearly the artist took pains to distill, and double-distill, his filial feeling. It isn't just the chalk and shadow complexion of the thing, but also the fact that he painted his mother in terribly still profile, as on a classical coin or gravestone. The paint itself, well sunk into the rough, unprepared canvas, is thin as thought. The prim, pensive, bonneted head appears very nearly translucent.

The picture's classic quietude stands in contrast to Whistler's own prickly swagger. The black drapery, gray floor, baseboard, footstool, figure, chair, gray wall, black-framed etchings, and drapery again, all form a revolving angular pattern which centers upon Mrs. Whistler's passive, softly shining hands. Here we see the first, tentative glimmer of the disengaged, purely "non-objective" painting style that Piet Mondrian, for example, was to practice. Every square inch of canvas seems alive in the knowledge of its own place and its peculiar part in the creation of an absolutely harmonious image.

Is there a living, breathing body under that black gown, a body which gave birth upon a time? The question is open, but the painting is closed—self-sufficient. "To me it is interesting as a picture of my mother," Whistler commented, "but can or ought the public to care about the identity of the portrait? It must stand or fall on its merits as an arrangement."

When the canvas was first shown in the Paris Salon of 1883, it didn't stand; it fell. "Whistler's Dead Mother," one critic called it. "This represents a poor woman trapped in a smoking apartment," another insisted. The artist himself ruefully concluded that for popularity's sake he ought to have painted in a glass of sherry at his mother's side, plus a Bible—"that book which, once set down, can never be taken up again."

Thomas Carlyle was among the few to admire Whistler's filial tribute. But when he commissioned the artist to portray him in similar style, the historian got an unpleasant surprise.

Staring, sweating, swearing, Whistler went at Carlyle's portrait with a paintbrush fastened to a three-foot broomhandle, plus his indispensable rubbing-out rag. The artist would lunge at his canvas, flick it, stagger back to a far corner of the studio, and briefly squint at his distinguished sitter. Then with a curse Whistler would leap forward again to wipe away whatever he had set down previously. This went on for weeks. Meanwhile Carlyle, who was growing lobster-pink with impatience, faded into the impeccably disposed mist and magic of Whistler's portrait.

There sits Carlyle, embalmed as it were: the hoary and crepuscular subject of *Arrangement in Gray and Black Number Two*. Although they were both created with great and intense labor by a genius at the top of his bent, the two "Arrangements" are of unequal weight. One "works"; the other doesn't. Why is this? Partly, at least, because Carlyle was not Whistler's father. "Whistler's Mother," after all, has to do with the door of the painter's own being.

> When at last, in all my storms, my whole self speaks, then there is a pause. The soul collects itself into pure silence and isolation—perhaps after much pain. The mind suspends its knowledge and waits. The psyche becomes strangely still.

So D. H. Lawrence observed in *Fantasia of the Unconscious* [192]. Those of us who were lucky used to have that experience when we buried our tear-stained faces in our mothers'—or perhaps our grandmothers'—skirts. Echoes of such a deep pause sigh through every pore of this thin-stretched, gravid, incredibly compelling work.

Despite his best effort to operate as a "transparent eyeball," in Ralph Waldo Emerson's famous phrase, the artist went deeper than he knew. At first his mother may appear to be a gray vacuum and ghost of shadows gone, but that's just the beginning. We're looking at a beautiful old witch who's laid aside her broomstick. She's the calm at the back of the north wind. She's got a pot of jasmine tea plus two or three ginger cookies prepared to offer Death this afternoon. He doesn't frighten her a bit, for she herself is much greater than he.

Whistler's Mother represents Oblivion: the dark of the moon. At her back stands invisible Radiance—the moon at the full—and Compassion, the starry matrix of humanity.

Demoiselles

I've been privileged to hold between my hands a hundred or more African carvings of the best quality. Those objects taught me—through the skin. Before commercialization set in, African masks and idols were carved for spirits to inhabit. They still cause one to sense the presence of invisible beings.

African carvers achieved extremely sophisticated effects by distorting, rigidifying, elasticating, minimalizing, and exaggerating forms. Also by mingling familiar features with abstract elements, by displacing parts, and substituting one for another. Finally, by freely employing holes, hollows, stick-thin or butterball projections, and acute or obtuse angles, all attuned to emotional tone. Their masks and idols were designed to appear in sacred places by starlight, and smoky firelight, accompanied by syncopated drumming, dancing, and the chanting of myths.

As one comes under the spell of this art at its best, one feels the pain of the spiritual beings represented. They suffer rebirth in carved wood form. Their rough passage through the portal between the worlds has been a burning, carbonizing, scarifying process. It's an expression of spiritual dynamics ripping through the usual order of things.

The same goes for a germinal canvas: Pablo Picasso's *Demoiselles d'Avignon*. He painted this in the spring of 1907, shortly after he and his friends Epstein, Derain, and Matisse had begun collecting African carvings from one or two curiosity shops on Montmartre. Short, barrel-chested, big-headed, with black cannon-mouth eyes, Picasso was himself a formidable figure. His birthplace was Malaga, a part of Spain long steeped in Moorish African culture.

The "Demoiselles" is by far the most important picture at Manhattan's Museum of Modern Art. Not for art historical reasons alone, but rather for its role in cultural evolution as a whole. Although lightly powdered with Paris taste, Picasso's painting announces the arrival of a new, African, presence in Western consciousness—a presence destined to release glittering hosts of unfamiliar images into modern dream-life.

According to an old Spanish proverb, Sunday calls for Mass in the morning, a bullfight in the afternoon, and a whorehouse at nightfall. Then are Picasso's knockabout "Demoiselles" really a rank, arboreal pride of prostitutes? Yes, said the artist to his friend Jaime Sabartes: "The picture represents to me a brothel in Avignon." But that's by no means all.

Nearly square at ninety-two by ninety-six inches, this canvas has a predominantly pyramidal composition. One seems to look up into it, as if from a kneeling posture. That, plus its flamelike lozenge arrangement of flattish planes, strongly recalls El

Greco's great *Opening of the Fifth Seal.* That's a canvas which long graced the Paris collection of Picasso's friend Zuloaga, who discovered it. Picasso became well acquainted with El Greco's masterpiece.

The Opening of the Fifth Seal indirectly addressed a contemporary horror: the Spanish Inquisition. El Greco's picture urged faith and courage; these terrors too would pass. His canvas is exalted in spirit. It illustrates the following passage from the Revelation of Saint John the Divine:

> And when he had opened the fifth seal, I saw under the altar the souls of them that were slain for the word of God, and for the testimony which they held: and they cried with a loud voice, saying, How long, O Lord, holy and true, dost thou not judge and avenge our blood on them that dwell on the earth? And ewhite robes were given unto every one of them; and it was said unto them, that they should rest yet for a little season. . . .

Inspired by African art, Picasso recast El Greco in a totally new mode. Despite its relatively carnal aspect, Picasso's canvas also deals in apocalyptic. Nakedly sheeted in heat lightning, the "Demoiselles" point ahead to two World Wars and the Nazi Holocaust—ashen passion, mass torture, and mushroom cloud. This image insists that we're no saints and never will be saved. Instead we are devoured, swallowed up in the forms of our own desire. We're caught and twirled in a whirlwind of human terror, lust, and dust. Picasso's message is damning in fact. But "bless relaxes," as William Blake remarked, whereas "damn braces."

Half-emergent from what seems a proscenium curtain of torn blue and brown, Picasso's five female nudes ambiguously semaphore. They're sensually contorted, half-crushed and splintery looking, deliciously painted in ochre and rose. Their violently rearranged faces, especially the pair on the right, resemble Ivory Coast masks. The "Demoiselles" appear to see, smell, and hear everything separately. Their eyes are frontal, even in profile. Their noses splay off sideways and their ears grow out of odd corners. Their lips are simple paintstrokes, unspeaking.

These five creatures form the fingers and thumb of an unseen hand whose cool, ivory-smooth clutch transports me to the mythosphere.

The island of Crete lies in the eastern Mediterranean Sea, nearly equidistant from Africa, Asia, and Europe—all three. El Greco came from there to settle in Toledo, Spain. According to pagan legend, Crete was the place where Rhea the titaness gave birth to Zeus. That was no easy delivery. They say that as the thunder god burst forth from her womb Rhea convulsively clutched the ground. Then, from the grooved earth ten finger-beings or "Dactyls" arose. The five at Rhea's right hand were youths, and they became the first blacksmiths. The five at her left hand were maidens, "Demoiselles," destined to become the first witches.

My mother groan'd! my father wept.
Into the dangerous world I leapt:

Helpless, naked, piping loud;
Like a fiend hid in a cloud.

Picasso's own birth was a drama reminiscent of those startling lines from William Blake's "Infant Sorrow," in his *Songs of Experience*.

He emerged bruise-blue, dead on arrival. After attempting with no success to revive the infant, the midwife laid him aside and turned her attention to saving the terribly and totally exhausted mother. The whole Picasso-Ruiz family was in attendance. The baby's uncle, Don Salvador Ruiz, happened to be a doctor. He lit a cigar. Bending hopefully above his wet, wrinkled, lifeless and abandoned relative on the table, Don Salvador puffed cigar smoke straight into the baby's open mouth.

It worked. Little Pablo coughed and howled. Wriggling he resembled a smoky flame. With furious reluctance he danced into life—like an African idol himself.

Nighthawk

"**J**ackson Pollock and Willem de Kooning have nothing to say."

After delivering that totally unjust judgment, Edward Hopper paused for a full minute or more, staring down at the floor between his shoes. "If they did," he concluded at last, "they wouldn't know how to say it."

"Both men paint images of flux," I suggested. "You can read whatever you like into those seismic openings of theirs. Exciting stuff."

"Humph!" Hopper said. That was his usual style of conversation. Never had I known so laconic a man.

We were in his Manhattan home: a fourth-floor walk-up at Number Three Washington Square North. The artist occupied the straight chair beside the old etching press he employed as a hat-rack. The tall windows at his back were violet with winter evening light, crossed by yellow lamplight reflections from within and flying snow outside.

"It's not hard to paint a design," Hopper told me dolefully. "Nor to paint a representation of something you can see. But to express a thought in painting—that is hard. Why? Because thought is fluid.

What you put on canvas is concrete, and this tends to direct the thought. The more you put on canvas, the less of your original thought remains."

That was by far the longest and most complex statement I had ever heard from Hopper's lips. Hunching forward in his chair he raised his right hand to eye-level. His eyes were nearly crossed with concentration upon an invisible something beyond his fingertips. He made me see it also: an imaginary paintbrush. Very carefully, now, the artist moved as if to touch the brush-tip to an imaginary canvas. He was doing fine until, at the moment of seeming contact, an invisible outside force joggled his elbow.

Getting into the spirit of things, I gasped with concern. Hopper sat back again, deadpan.

Born to a storekeeping family in Nyack, New York, Hopper doggedly pursued his art career with almost no encouragement from any quarter. Like diamonds, this man's high art was produced under blind, stony pressure. Until the age of forty, he made a meager living as a commercial illustrator. "I'd walk around the block a couple of times before going in," he once confessed, "wanting the job for money and at the same time hoping to hell I wouldn't get the lousy thing."

Gravity and sparingness are qualities deep in the Puritan grain. Emily Dickinson possessed them; so did Charles Sheeler, Robert Frost, and Georgia O'Keeffe. But Edward Hopper was perhaps the gravest and sparest of the lot. His chirpy wife Jo did the smiling and chatting for them both.

Not until 1955, when he was in his seventies, did Hopper begin to receive the attention his non-commercial art had always merited. In that year he was awarded a Gold Medal for Painting by the American Academy of Arts and Letters. There was unconcealed bitterness in Hopper's one-word acceptance speech:

"Thankyou."

"Recognition doesn't mean so much," the old gentleman confided to me next day. "You never get it when you need it."

Paintings are supposed to be silent of course. Some are more so than others. Hopper's have a bell-jar sort of silence about them. Not a sound, and yet you feel that if you were to touch a Hopper canvas with a tuning-fork it might well produce a barely audible vibration. His whole oeuvre seethes with low-voltage electric charges. It coruscates with paradoxically dark brilliance.

"In every work of genius we recognize our own rejected thoughts. They come back to us with a certain alienated majesty." So Ralph Waldo Emerson observed, and Hopper's paintings bear that out. He deflects our own rejected thoughts back upon ourselves, with interest. Something which one had glimpsed a hundred times in passing from the corner of one's eye, or thought about a thousand times without ever pausing to reconsider, proves arresting after all.

Tearless nostalgia, the ache of loneliness, and finally the sense of romance just beyond reach, inform Hopper's creative work. Each of his great canvases is narrowly but brilliantly staged, emptied of trivial details, and subtly distorted for dramatic impact. Each one tells a wordless story, but they're not illustrations of anything. Rather, they project strangely splendid insights into secret America.

Consider his *Nighthawks*, for example. This canvas, at the Chicago Art Institute, dates from 1942. We're out near a city corner, at the midnight hour, looking across the street and in through the plate glass window of a bright-lit fast-food joint. Hopper may well have passed a place like this on his frequent prowls around Greenwich Village, but he had his own means of transposing the scene to a legendary realm. Thus he enlarged the empty pavement and the dark building, so that they seem broadly sweeping gestures of the night itself.

Contrastingly, the four figures at the counter inside appear small, crisp, courageous, and half-conscious of their isolation—marooned in light. The customer with his back to the street sits gazing across at the tensely close couple opposite, and the priestly counterman in his starched white vestments. These four figures all display the same angular, dimly repressed body-language.

This awkward stiffness is theirs, not Hopper's, yet the artist himself abjured gesture as a general rule. The flamboyance of the surrealists and the abstract expressionists alike repelled him. His own art has the stillness of a dreamer in bed. It doesn't express emotion; rather, it projects a mood peculiar to this artist alone. The mood is bleak and yet tender at the same time. It conveys a quality of casting about for one knows not what, like an inchworm at the end of a twig. "Self-seeking" was a synonym for selfishness in Hopper's time, and generally frowned upon. Yet Hopper insisted that he was in fact "a self-seeker."

Like every other mid-century artist of note, Hopper was naturally aware of psychoanalytic theory. It probably occurred to him that the four silently poised "Nighthawks" could symbolize distinct aspects of his own psyche. It's possible to read the painted scene as a mandala, a light-filled "center" in the dark of the painter's "unconscious" or dream-life. Thus the four figures could be interpreted as Jungian "archetypes": Shadow, Anima, Wise Old Man, and Ego, respectively. One might also see them as psychic functions: Feeling, Sensing, Thinking, and Intuiting. Finally, they bring to mind the four "humors" of ancient lore: Sanguine, Phlegmatic, Melancholic, and Choleric.

But archetypes, functions, and humors are not self.

Looking at *Nighthawks,* I sense an invisible fifth participant who hovers on our side of the street. A passerby like us, he observes the action from the dark, and in through the plate glass, with appreciative and yet rather terrible detachment. Darkly shimmering, mercurial and soon gone again is the artist's self, the actual nighthawk.

Persephone in Missouri

Thomas Hart Benton once confessed that during his Missouri boyhood he used to "get fascinated with the nature of a fence post, a bush, a rock, or a ripple of water. . . . I would pass from an abstracted study of one of these into a long and, as far as I could ever explain it, an empty reverie. This psychological failing developed long before I ever thought of myself as an artist. It was a thing that my Dad could never understand. He had plenty of abstracted moments himself, but they were never of a kind that would make him miss a train because he was interested in the smoke of its engine."

"Psychological failing," is tough-guy doubletalk, of course. "Empty reverie" vis-à-vis the objective world actually invites wisdom. Every young child learns from nature herself to practice this. Reverie is childhood's main access to understanding. Instead of reaching for facts and ideas, one empowers the thing in itself to speak, to signify something beyond.

Artists of Benton's kind keep on doing that all their lives long.

If Benton at play was a bourbon-swollen mini-swashbuckler (and no mean maestro of the harmonica), Benton at work was a paragon of large-minded concentration. And if Benton's art was energetic, blunt, deliberately theatrical, it was also profoundly worked out. He used to begin with sketches and then construct a wax or clay model of the scene he meant to represent, painting monochrome shadows and highlights on the model itself. Bronzino, Georges de la Tour, and Francisco Zurburan are said to have done likewise. Benton always composed the final picture from his model, not life. He dedicated himself to a particular kind of artificial reality which painting alone can project.

No wonder "jumping cubes, cockeyed tables, blue bowls and bananas" made Benton savage with laughter. As for pure abstractions, he dismissed those outright. "Without sustained effectiveness on the mind," Benton explained, "they cannot have sustained life—even for artists."

Since his death in 1976, Benton's stock has risen steadily. When Kansas City's Nelson-Atkins Museum of Art paid $2,500,000 for his *Rape of Persephone*, they got a bargain: a major work by one of Missouri's three most creative sons (the other two: Samuel Clemens and Count Basie). But local church fathers, led by the Reverend Loren Green, expressed outrage at the Nelson-Atkins Museum's purchase. Others rose to defend it; witness the following limerick which appeared in a Kansas City newspaper:

There once was a preacher named Green
who thought Persephone obscene.
He knew what was lewd,

this psalm-singing prude.
If it doesn't wear clothes it ain't clean.

The picture shows a farmer's daughter—or perhaps a young country schoolteacher—unself-con-
sciously lounging, stretched out like an unwitting
sacrifice between earth and sky, down by the creek.
She's naked, long-boned, slim-fleshed, still gleaming from her swim. It's all too easy for a man to
view this cool, somewhat virginal figure with con-
cupiscent complacency. But this is no saloon nude.
Persephone's a vulnerable Missouri girl, subject to
goosepimples from the September chill.

Afternoon shadows lengthen within the frame.
There may be bugs or even snakes about. Shouldn't
Persephone watch out? One senses trouble afoot,
violence in the moist and dusty air. And here it
comes. Belatedly, one notices a horny-handed,
cucumber-nosed old farmer, a viperish son of the
soil, slithering dolefully up from behind. That's a
human stand-in for the pagan god Hades, who
seized the original Persephone down into his
deathly realm under the earth.

Hades gathered all things, great and small, beneath his hospitable sway. The god's beard glittered
with diamond dust. His eyes were cherry-red. He
had pomegranate testicles and a tumescently
twitchy penis. The dark monarch was formidably
affectionate in cold weather, an indefagitable
fornicator.

Throughout the autumn and winter, Benton's
Persephone will lie constrained among the gem-
beds, arrowheads, rusted plows, seed-pots, snakes,
tomahawks, moles, maggots, veining metals, skulls,

centipedes, shell-casings, worms, pale sprouts, and rough root-forms of Nether-Missouri. Then finally the late-March thaw, followed by the showers of April, will release her—virgin once more—into the upper world and the light of the sun.

Benton himself projected a swaggeringly masculine persona. Yet in order to create this picture he must have played Persephone's role in the theater of his own soul. Note that the soul itself is neither male nor female; it's presexual. Let gender-driven agendas come and go. Myth can't be understood, let alone reimagined and reshaped, other than mythically.

Talk in the Dark

God gave King Solomon "an understanding heart." Ordinary people sometimes get one too, but just what function does "an understanding heart" perform?

Unless my emotions are irradiated with light and cool thought-processes, I'm body-bound to behave in a reactive, nonsensical and violent fashion. Unless my thoughts are imbued with dark and warm feeling-processes on the other hand, I'm brain-bound to barren slyness and melancholy speculation. So an "understanding heart," as I imagine this, would be a beautifully developed and balanced organ situated—like the physical heart—in the wellspring of one's circulatory system. Thus placed it would mediate between light and dark, warm and cool, the conscious brain and the unconscious liver, spleen, etcetera; vortexing and as it were tasting the entire mix from moment to moment.

As Mephistopheles remarked to Faust: "Blood is a very special fluid."

Washington Irving was no King Solomon, and no Shakespeare either, but the first universally admired American writer did approach the world in a heartfelt way. Irving's eye commanded past shadowlands and contemporary distances alike. He pondered and conjured both in gently affectionate style. If his foreground scenes sparkle with vivid and precise touches, his middle-distances offer long, vague undulations of feeling-thought. He was a sweet-souled wizard in the deliberate ordering of words, sentences, paragraphs, and indeed whole pages at a go, whose genius fills one's imagination with deep, rich confusion of not-quite-song.

1783 was the year the Treaty of Paris capped the triumph of the American Revolution. It was also the year of Washington Irving's birth. The eleventh child of a Scots Covenanter merchant couple, he found welcome as the last baby of the family. New York was then a bustling port city with a population of less than thirty thousand clustered between Wall Street and the Battery. As Irving remembered:

> I was always fond of visiting new scenes, and observing strange characters and manners. Even when a mere child I began my travels, and made many tours into foreign parts and unknown regions of my native city, to the frequent alarm of my parents, and emolument of the town-crier. As I grew into boyhood, I extended the range of my observations. My holiday afternoons were spent in rambles about the surrounding country. . . . I even journeyed one long summer's day to the summit of the most distant hill, whence I stretched my eye over many a mile of "terra incognita," and was astonished to find how vast a globe I inhabited.

That "most distant" boyhood expedition was probably to Murray Hill, the present site of Grand Central Station.

Some affinity is to be expected between an author and his most famous creation. Doesn't Irving the boy resemble Rip Van Winkle in character? Rip loved wandering the wilds with his faithful hound and fowling-piece, or sitting slouched on the bench before the village inn, "telling endless sleepy stories about nothing."

In Irving's New York, practicality was the order of the day. "The very words learning, education, taste and talents were unheard-of," he recalled. "A bright genius was an animal unknown, and a blue-stocking lady would have been regarded with as much wonder as a horned frog or a fiery dragon."

Rip Van Winkle's long, long sleep amounted to a little death; his very name suggests the initials for "Rest in Peace." Yet he eventually awoke to a new world where, after all, things went on as before only better. And in Irving's case the "bright genius," unrecognized at home, awoke to find himself a celebrity abroad. As he observed:

> It has been a matter of marvel to my European readers that a man from the wilds of America should express himself in tolerable English. I was looked upon as something new and strange in literature, a kind of demi-savage with a feather in his hand instead of on his head.

The success of his quill pen enabled Irving to travel widely and to build a hospitable home a few miles up the Hudson River from Manhattan. "Sunnyside" lay within strolling distance of Sleepy Hollow, the Headless Horseman's haunt. The mansion boasted half a dozen chimney-hearths and old-Dutch crow-stepped gables. The deep, shady porches, festooned with honeysuckle and trumpet creepers, overlooked panoramic river views. The opulent interior glowed with Moorish carpets and gleamed with copper, silk, and ceramic tile souvenirs of the author's adventures in Spain, along with weapons and Native American artifacts he'd picked up in the Wild West.

Sunnyside's tower library contained a Morocco-bound, twenty-volume edition of Irving's lifework. This massive, excellently crafted oeuvre has long since sunk beneath the tumultuous ocean of world literature. Just two slim paper ships, namely *Rip Van Winkle* and *The Legend of Sleepy Hollow*, remain afloat.

Both tales are supple, witty, sensuous, and fraught with irony of the gentlest, most humane sort. They intermingle the sound of far-bowled thunder with the sight of "odd-looking personages playing at nine-pins." They contrast the jolly tinkle of tankards to the persistent thrum of pursuing hooves. They set the screaming and chattering of a blue jay, "in his gay light-blue coat and white under-clothes," against the "drowsy undertone with which men talk in the dark."

Like fish in water, our minds move and disport themselves in electrochemical tides, abstract lakes, and chambers of the fabulous. Meanwhile we develop outwardly silent circuits—from heart to larynx to tongue, and back again—which broadcast a continuous private drama. Then, too, we tell each other stories all the time. A more or less continuous narrative, both covert and overt, constitutes the main product of one's waking life. It demonstrates the braided flow of experience and legend.

Words are as natural to us as song is to the thrush. The smallest birds are the loveliest singers, and ordinary people often have extraordinary tales to tell. Washington Irving's two famous stories bring the ordinary into concert with the mythic. His "understanding heart" is their strength.

The Unpaintable

The arts empower one to circle backward and "drop in" at various points along the human adventure. Often we sense that we've been there before. That's one more reason why art and literature ought never to be regarded as "frill subjects." They body forth the story of our race.

Like the eighth century of our era, the sixteenth was also fraught with religious wars. Pieter Brueghel the Elder (1525–1569) suffered in consequence, and the conflict shaped his art. Brueghel's head was careful yet his heart could not be silent. He revealed the evils of his day indirectly, through legendary parallels. His last instructions were to destroy some of the pictures he had made, lest they fall into the hands of the Inquisition. The artist painted with miniaturist care on large panels of well-seasoned wood, using gesso, egg tempera, and thin oil glazes. He meant his work to last. But on the other hand Brueghel was determined to protect his wife and sons from posthumous vengeance upon himself.

Among Brueghel's comrades was the renowned geographer Ortelius, who became one among sixty thousand Lowland emigrees to England. Accused of Copernican Heresy, Ortelius was forced to flee Flanders for university life at Cambridge. Upon learning of Brueghel's death, he composed a eulogy stating: "All Brueghel's art contains more intelligence than painting." Darkly, Ortelius added: "He painted many things that are really unpaintable."

Brueghel had no peer, and no artistic heirs. His sons Jan Brueghel and Pieter Brueghel the Younger were minor makers of pleasant pictures: wall-furniture, in effect. The elder Brueghel's only spiritual twin and fellow titan of the northern Renaissance was a dramatist: William Shakespeare. Both men were reputed to be humbly born and yet displayed a more than kingly quality. They resembled Socrates in that respect and in another one as well. Namely their uncanny capacity for drawing one's own thoughts into the light.

John Milton praised "sweetest Shakespeare, fancy's child," for warbling "his native Wood-notes wild." Karel van Mander, the Vasari of the north, seemed similarly condescending to Brueghel. "In a wonderful manner," van Mander enthused, "Nature found and seized the man who in his turn was destined to seize her so magnificently, when, in an obscure village of the Brabant she chose from among the peasants, as a delineator of peasants, the witty and gifted Pieter Brueghelo."

That's so far off the mark it leads one to suspect that van Mander meant to protect the master. Brueghel was not a "delineator of peasants" alone but of the whole world about him, both as it existed then and in the myth dimension. Besides, nobody can "seize nature"; we can't even leap out of her lap. That's why we'll never perceive reality as a whole.

Reality is the total experience of the entire world. Nature, in a word. But when you run that definition backward it scans rather differently. Because, from a pragmatic viewpoint, nature is experience. Only by asking questions and axing preconceptions, letting the chips fall where they may, can one begin to discern what actually happens. Only by practicing curiosity and concern for others will one ever comprehend one's own part in the play.

I mean the mythic drama wherein each person must perforce participate.

This is Brueghel's unspoken philosophy, and the subtext of all his art. Every great Brueghel panel seems to extend out and around the viewer, then close in from behind. You become part of the pictured scene, and that's unsettling. Something, somewhere in the image, seems to be hidden from your eyes. Why should this be? You stay and stay, look and look again, grappling with the mystery of it all until—out of the blue—you may discover what's going on. Nothing has changed, except that now your own part in the action stands revealed.

Why did van Mander slyly add a Spanish ending to Brueghel's name, calling him "Brueghelo"? Spain ruled over the Netherlands at the time. Might this artist have been the unacknowledged son of a conquering Spanish nobleman, perhaps a "Prince of the Church"? The historian Gustav Gluck remarks that portraits of Brueghel "show him as the complete townsman, modishly dressed, with the long well-trimmed beard particularly favored by artists of his day, and with noble, thoughtful, rather melancholy features which seem to reveal a highly cultured mind."

Most of Brueghel's major panels speak subversively to crucial issues of the painter's own day. Yet the artist's fierce, radical–Christian overtones are almost never talked about. They're painfully disturbing, and some would say parochial. In any case, people have always blocked them out. Here's the story behind his *Massacre of the Innocents*, from the Gospel according to Saint Matthew:

> There came wise men from the east to Jerusalem, saying, Where is he that is born King of the Jews? for we have seen his star in the east, and are come to worship him.

The coming of the Wise Men profoundly disturbed King Herod, who reigned over Palestine with the backing of imperial Rome. Herod's shining Temple on the Holy Rock of Jerusalem, his "Antonia Fortress" in the same city, his Machpelah shrine at Hebron, and his personal country palaces at Samaria, Jericho, Masada, Machaerus, and Bethlehem, not to mention his far-flung monuments at Damascus, Byblos, and Antioch, made him one of the greatest builders the world had ever seen. Now, however, he was old and ill. He suffered from delusions, depressions, and episodes of vicious violence. For example, he put one of his wives and two of his sons to death. Such was the Herod who commanded his visitors to carry on, find the newborn King, and then report back, "so that I may come and worship him also."

The Wise Men followed their star to Bethlehem, where Herod himself would be laid to rest within a few years:

And when they were come into the house,
they saw the young child with Mary his
mother, and fell down and worshipped him;
and when they had opened their treasures,
they presented unto him gifts; gold, and
frankincense, and myrrh. And being warned
of God in a dream that they should not return
to Herod, they departed into their own country another way. And when they were departed, behold, the angel of the Lord
appeareth to Joseph in a dream, saying Arise,
and take the young child and his mother, and
flee into Egypt; and be thou there until I bring
thee word; for Herod will seek the young
child to destroy him.

And so it was. No sooner had the holy family
fled than Herod's troops appeared, scoured the
Bethlehem region for babies under the age of two,
and slaughtered them all.

In Rama was there a voice heard,
Lamentation, and weeping, and great
mourning,
Rachel weeping for her children,
And would not be comforted, because they
are not.

The *Massacre of the Innocents* puts an urgent
contemporary gloss on the Gospel story. This
overtly polemical masterpiece shows Walloon redcoats butchering baby after baby on the shining
snow of a Flemish village. In Brueghel's day traitor-
ous home-troops were performing the Duke of
Alba's work, implementing the Spanish conqueror's

"Edict of Blood." (Alba boasted of having executed eighteen thousand "heretics and rebels.")

Brueghel favored aloof perspectives, floating out-of-body, as it were. Confronted with this picture I find myself gazing down at the massacre from tree-top level. I see the babies being slaughtered. I share their mothers' desperation. I yearn to reach through to the murderous soldiers' hearts. If only one could teach them compassion! Pausing in mid-slaughter, certain Walloons look around and up. They know they haven't found Jesus yet. Where can he be? Having illuminated history's icy, blood-streaked current, Brueghel makes an airy gyration which leads up into the trees to reach my eye-level. In a nearby treetop there's an empty nest. The bird has flown, apparently. The soldiers look up at the nest; then slowly their eyes shift in my direction—outside the picture—but they don't see me.

Perched like a magpie, beyond the soldiers' ken, I preen my unaccustomed wings while brooding over the image as a whole. So much death, all for the sake of one small life, one great promise, a Child. Now it strikes me that Jesus must be somewhere nearby. Safely hidden from the Walloons. From me as well. Just where might he be hiding? On the snow, or in the air? Is he cold?

Now one particular soldier looks up again—straight at me. Why? What have I got to do with all this? I'm not hiding anyone. In my heart, has the Child ever found a nest?

· PART THREE ·

The Pursuit of Virtue

Introduction

We all depend upon each other. Also upon the plants and animals. Not to mention the life-bestowing conglomerates: Earth, Air, Fire, and Water. Every living person is part of a give and take network which entails considerable suffering as well as joy. This largely mysterious ambiance constitutes nature as experienced by—and affected by—you and me. One's own self is the center, so each person has plenty to do by way of loving and working for the common good. Avoiding our human obligations is by no means impossible, but it carries considerable risk. Such as crinkling up like an autumn leaf; dying on the inside.

> I slept, and dreamed that life was Beauty;
> I woke, and found that life was Duty.

As a mythologist and art historian I have been accused of pulling the covers over my head and going back to sleep in order to "dream of beauty." It's true that art and myth can be extremely beautiful and seductive. But that's a quality, not a purpose. Great art pleases but it also signifies. And the pervading purpose of our mythmaking ancestors, all down the centuries, has been to awaken us.

All men and women require to be roused, every now and then, from habit-bound, lightly dozing ways. We need release from pillow-pounding, pre-conceived opinions. Our better selves yearn to see things—including our own strengths and short-comings—as they really are. We could use a cold shower, as it were, and many myths offer just that. In general it's fair to say that myth educates and instructs, especially about ethics. That is, about appropriate behavior in a sometimes nightmare world.

> Virgin Gaia had a son,
> Ouranos, the Atmosphere,
> to match her own dimension.
>
> He covered her,
> and their first-born
> was Okeanos, Deep-swirler.

So the Greek poet Hesiod proclaimed nearly three thousand years ago. We learned much the same thing in school, minus the poetry, of course. Didn't this planet extrude her own atmosphere and interact with that to conceive the streaming ocean? It's curious, and should be humbling, that "evolution myths" often foreshadow the dry "scientific findings" of today.

Old-fashioned science rather grudgingly agrees that our planet extruded the atmosphere, veiled herself in the Seven Seas, gave birth to life, and very gradually nursed the biosphere along to its present point of complexity. But traditional scientists still insist that this whole process was and is accidental. Plants are totally uncaring, they explain. Animals have no purpose beyond preserving and propagating their own kind. Complex consciousness occurs only in *homo sapiens.* So the world as we know it can only have come into existence via the blind, accumulative force of chance.

James Lovelock is one of the many contemporary scientists to question these tired assumptions. Like a latter-day Druid, Lovelock addresses the world from a long-denuded Devon dale which he's taken pains to plant with some twenty thousand ash, elder, beech, and oak seedlings. His home forest is rooting well, and the same goes for Lovelock's leading idea. Earthlife is by no means an agglomeration of accidents, he contends. The biosphere lives and breathes. It's a consciously evolving and self-regulating network of mineral, vegetable, and animal constituents.

Lovelock outlined this basic premise one day while walking across a moor with the novelist William Golding. "Well," he said, "what do you think?" Golding replied that he liked the notion of bringing Gaia back into play. "Yes," Lovelock enthused, "gyres are an important part of the picture, mathematically."

"You misheard me," Golding said. "I'm not talking about expanding spirals, but about the Greek earth goddess: Gaia!"

The oneness of the biosphere relates to the timelessness of the mythosphere. Viewed as a whole, our home planet is profoundly harmonious and like an age-old, blue-mantled divinity. And that's how she appears in myth after myth. European, African, Asiatic and Native American legend alike confirm her beneficent sway.

When and if Lovelock's scientific yet anciently reverent and wise approach to the planet prevails, what will happen? It's safe to say that weapon-builders, vivisectionists, and the fast-growing new breed of geneticists, will feel less blithe about their activities.

Herodotus, the first and liveliest of all historians, tells this story in his "Persian Wars." The Persian Emperor Xerxes became royally annoyed with the waters of the Hellespont, whose glittering current separates northwestern Asia Minor from southeastern Europe. Xerxes hated the strait for daring to obstruct his march against Greece. Therefore, at his express command she was steamily branded with hot irons and then subjected to three hundred splashy lashes of the bullwhip, while being scolded as follows:

> Oh, salt and bitter stream, your master lays this punishment upon you for injuring him, who never injured you; but Xerxes the King will cross you, with or without your permission. No man sacrifices to you, and you deserve neglect by your acrid and muddy manners.

Herodotus calls that "A highly presumptuous way of addressing the Hellespont, and typical of a barbarous nation."

Having finally managed to bridge the Hellespont by means of boats bound together broadside, gunwale to gunwale, Xerxes did invade Greece. He led the greatest army ever seen up to that time, a force drawn from the far reaches of his empire. Bactrian bowmen with arrows of cane, Ethiopians in lionskins, Red Sea lancers with crane-skin shields, Libyans bearing fire-hardened javelins, Scythians in fawn-skin boots, Psydian swordsmen wearing horned helmets and crimson leggings, Caspian cavalry armed with daggers and lassoes, and Bedoins on camels, plus a vast naval continent spearheaded by 1,207 Egyptian, Phoenician, Syrian, and Cypriot triremes, came swarming toward Athens.

Clearly, the Greeks didn't stand a chance against Xerxes. Like the hayseed, raggle-taggle musketmen of the American Colonies against Great Britain's redcoats, or like the black-pyjamaed North Vietnamese against the United States, they seemed hopelessly outmanned. Yet Xerxes was turned back in the naval battle of Salamis, with tremendous losses. As Lord Byron described it:

> The king sat on the rocky brow
> Which looks o'er sea-born Salamis;
> And ships, by thousands, lay below,
> And men in nations;—all were his!
> He counted them at break of day—
> And when the sun set, where were they?

Hubris, overweening pride, has always been the engine that drives human tragedy. Aeschylus' *The Persians* (in G. M. Cookson's translation) drives that point home:

> This earth, this Asia, wide as east from west,
> Mourns—empty—of her manhood
> dispossessed.
> Xerxes the King led forth his war-array!

Xerxes the King hath cast his host away!
Xerxes the King (O King unwise!)
Steered in the wake of doom his orient argosies!

The main message encoded in Greek drama is simple: practice reverence. Yet the pagan Greeks were never ones to genuflect. When they worshiped, they did so standing erect. Pious posturing and eating humble pie were repulsive to them. They gagged on apologies. The reverence that their oracles and poets sought to inculcate was the true opposite of hubris—as "humility" is not.

Being mere babes in the wood, we naturally reach out for comfort, sustenance, and all the knowledge we can get. But wonderingly, reverently, is the best way. "Letting the forest think through us," as my mother used to say.

One afternoon when I was only ten, my father turned up at school. I'd never seen him there before. He carried a leather case, a "makeup kit," as he explained. His purpose: to paste a full red beard and mustache on my face, with "spirit gum." The ether fumes had me reeling, half-sick. Meanwhile the school auditorium filled up with parents. They had come to watch us children perform an ancient Greek comedy: *The Frogs* of Aristophanes.

The teachers fussed around, getting us ready to go on. Proud of my boyish strength, I'd volunteered for the role of Herakles. Lacking a lionskin, they draped me, toga style, in a blanket softly dotted with leopard spots. Moodily flexing my slender muscles I strode up and down the dressing room with the blanket dragging at my heels. A giant club was thrust into my hands. Roughly hewn from a fallen tree branch, it seemed pretty heavy. In fact the club was taller than myself. However, I took this comic prop for a compliment.

My brief dramatic turn went pretty well, I thought, right up until my exit scene. While backing away upstage, I somehow caught my club between the cardboard columns of a temple portico. The entire set crashed down. That was a showstopper. The assembled parents howled with delight.

I couldn't understand what they were laughing about.

Every tribe and nation displays fierce hungers and furious pretensions which metamorphose from age to age. Each generation in turn puts out more flags, sunset-silks of ever-receding glamour. Our legendary heroes change their minds, their weapons, and their ways, meanwhile, down the centuries. Herakles, for example.

The earliest Homeric Hymns celebrate Herakles in armor, as a dazzling demigod. He dared challenge Ares, the pig-eyed Olympian, to single combat. Moreover, he succeeded in painfully wounding the deathless one. He even scratched the battle-deity's stony and unstoppable heart.

With the founding of Greek colonies across the sea in Italy and North Africa, Herakles became a pioneer huntsman. His knightly panoply was next to useless in the wilderness, so the Sicilian poet Stesichorus re-equipped Herakles with the attributes by which he's still best recognized: a short, double-curved bow, a quiver of arrows, a cudgel carved from a wild olive branch, and a lionskin costume.

The Agora Museum in Athens holds an archaic fist-size sculptured head of Herakles the huntsman. His eyes are astonishingly wide, whereas he has a narrow smile. He brings to mind William Butler Yeats' line:

A terrible beauty is born.

In this case the beauty seems born from the jaws of a lion, which Herakles has killed and flayed. The lion's muzzle serves the hero as a sort of helmet. One feels that he'd keep dry in a deluge, and cool in a conflagration. He's not altogether human.

Pindar, the poet laureate of the ancient Olympic Games, transformed the hero once again. Thanks to him, Herakles became a quick, sleek-muscled, gentleman athlete. Effortless grace replaced the primordial power which he possessed of old. Thus an early classical relief in the museum at Delphi shows a bare-handed Herakles leaping to seize the sacred doe of Artemis. As Pindar says, he "made the right moves at the right moments."

But nobody does it without help. At Olympia there's a metope which portrays Herakles bearing, or seeming to bear, the whole weight of heaven for Atlas the Titan. Behind him stands the virgin goddess of wisdom: Athena. In fact the main burden rests upon the resistless palm of the divine maiden's hand. The Louvre Museum holds a red-figured amphora dating from the end of the sixth century B.C. It shows Herakles about to capture Hades' watchdog. Very gently, the hero bends to stroke one of Cerberus' three snarling snouts. Here again Athena makes her presence felt, standing by impassively.

I've trailed Herakles' legend around many an Attic vase. Their clay mouths seem to whisper coldly, like the reeds and sandy currents of the river Achelous—which the hero wrestled upon a time. Half-naked, thick-thighed, flat-bellied, and long-fingered, Herakles passes by. He moves impersonally, like a well-oiled wrestler dusted with sand. That's how the Greek vase painters pictured him: as fleet and sharp as a shadow thrown by the desert sun.

Victorious against the Persians, swollen with imperial pride, and consequently paranoid, Athens needed reform. So the great playwrights of her golden age set themselves to remold municipal consciousness from within. The supremely sensitive political leader Pericles promoted this. He pushed a law through his Assembly whereby the citizens were paid jury duty fees for free attendance at their own theater. There they found Herakles recast by the tragedian Euripides, who presented him as a jolly boor on one occasion and again as a profound madman.

Sophocles, more orthodox in his thinking, took pains to right the record. He put Herakles on stage as a severely ideal figure and guardian of the good. That concept prevailed. Warning signs appeared on thousands of gateposts: "Herakles is Inside."

The Romans called him "Hercules," and that's how he's appeared in children's stories and schoolbooks ever since. Stoic philosophers of the Roman period credited their austere cult to Hercules' influence. He was the first philosopher, they said. Medieval astrologers redefined Hercules as a sun symbol, laboring through each of the Twelve Signs of the Zodiac in turn. The Renaissance humanists made him their champion, as one who asserted personal independence in the very teeth of fate.

Finally, William Blake found Hercules "a receptacle of Wisdom, a sublime Energizer."

He's always been my own hero. In one of my first books I presented him as a hydraulic engineer. He was the "Water Tamer," who invented irrigation, sanitation, and flood control while setting his face against arbitrary authority, hypocrisy, and the madness of human sacrifice. To me, his virtues seemed almost prophetically American.

It's true that our nation can look back upon a Herculean, harshly tasked yet largely glorious history. At present, however, we are experiencing bloat and pain. I'm reminded of a late-classical marble figure which the Athenian sculptor Lycon copied from Lysippus. It stands looming gloomily, some ten feet tall, in the National Archeological Museum at Naples. Nude, the champion leans upon a ponderous club over which he's draped his lionskin.

This "mature" Herakles or Hercules holds his head stiffly bowed in thought. He resembles a bull-necked, bone-weary bath attendant who has witnessed much corruption and rubbed the evil down. As if warped by the bath steam, his giant frame stoops heavily. Disgusted with his masters, sick at heart, he shrinks inside his aging, arthritic yoke and harness of muscles. Meanwhile he holds one hand behind his back, clutching a last ephemeral prize: the golden apples of the Western Isles, the Hesperides.

America possesses huge, God-given power to heal or else pollute, to teach or else murder, to solace or else destroy. The world grows smaller, meanwhile, and it's one place for all. Do we carry too big a stick? Will we pull down the stage set?

The Quicken-Tree Palace

A Robin Red breast in a Cage
Puts all Heaven in a Rage.

When I first came across those lines from William Blake, I presumed to regard the couplet as an example of "poetic license." But it stuck, anyhow.

What drives the courtship rituals, the mating practices, the parental imperatives, the family life, the playful activities, the conflicts, the hunting and gathering strategies, the convocations, and the distant migrations, of birds, bugs, and beasts? "Animal instinct" is the answer generally given. But that's just a phrase used to conceal modern humanity's almost total ignorance of the subject.

We do certain things instinctively, that's true. However, most of what we do is determined by what we've learned from fellow humans over the years. In other words, it's a question of nature plus culture. The same principle probably applies throughout the animal kingdom. We can't see it because we fail to respect or even recognize most animal societies. The totemic wisdom of our ancestors is gone. The sea-fowl flies to her nest by the shore, and the lion lies down in his lair, while all alone the human animal sits grandly at the head of the table, grinding its stony teeth in heedless majesty.

Marine biologist Katy Payne and three associates recently completed a fifteen-year study of aural communications both within and between humpback whale communities which freely disport across many thousands of miles in the cradle of the deep. Wide-ranging research convinced the team that whales are indeed carriers of culture like ourselves. As Dr. Payne explains:

> For reasons we do not understand, singing is a complex behavior in humpback whales. Their long, complex songs evolve rapidly over time. The songs are learned, and the changes passed on by learning. Whale songs include structures and devices we find in human song and poetry—for instance, rhyming. Singing is always present when humpback whales are courting. Why they sing such elaborate songs, why the songs change, and where the changes come from, is not known. We don't know how humpback whales choose their winter singing grounds . . . We know even less about most other marine mammals. We have no way to assess how much "play" there is in each aspect of their lives, from their basic demography and distribution to their cultural behavior. We only know that acoustic communication is involved at every level.

Do whale songs have mythic content? Why not? Why shouldn't humpbacked Homers blow, or blue Ovids melodiously sob, or dolphin Dantes divinize, or great gray Shakespeares go shimmering throughout the Seven Seas? I don't say this is actually the case. I do say that there's not one shred of evidence against it.

> I shall not ask Jean Jacques Rousseau,
> If birds confabulate or no.

So wrote William Cowper. And Ludwig van Beethoven remarked that friendly yellowhammers and cuckoos had helped compose his Pastoral Symphony.

My ears tell me that birds also are carriers of culture. It's commonly asserted that they sing merely to establish territorial rights, or sometimes to attract a mate. But anyone who enjoys sitting on a log in a forest in spring, just listening, knows there's more to birdsong. Much more. While silently participating in the near and far of a wild bird concert for an hour, or two, or three, one comes to sense its interactive complexity.

> That's the wise thrush; he sings each song twice over,
> Lest you should think he never could recapture
> The first fine careless rapture!

—Lighthearted lines by Robert Browning, who listened better than most of us, and wrote better than he listened. In all the communicative arts, "careless rapture" is a consummation devoutly to be wished. Achieving it requires extreme discipline, structurally attuned to well-understood and mutually agreed-upon parameters.

That's what musician Charlie ("Bird") Parker, for example, had going for him. One cannot fully appreciate Parker's genius without comprehending bebop, yet one enjoys it anyhow. The same goes for Italian opera. One doesn't require a program, or even familiarity with the language, to relish that. Although we miss a lot, we're hardly aware of the fact.

Deep in a green grove of beech trees, birches, and English oaks, I'm enjoying the wild concert. Yet I'm as deaf to avian culture as the birds are blithely ignorant of mine.

King Finn of the Fena went hunting across Limerick with his best warriors. They were enjoying a peaceful picnic on the western slope of Knockfierna, when a sorcerer named Midac rode up and recited the following verse:

> I saw to the south
> a silver queen
> on a crystal couch,
> in a gown of green,
> with sprightly young
> beneath her skin.
> She's slow, yet swift.
> Who is it, Finn?

Upon reflection King Finn replied: "The queen you saw is the river Boyne, which flows by the south side of the Brugh which belongs to Angus. Her crystal couch consists of the river's sandy bed. Her green robe is the grassy plain of Bregia, through which she meanders. Her children, whom you discerned through her transparent skin, are the speckled salmon, the pretty trout, and all the other fish that swim there. Her current is leisurely, and yet in seven years those same waters circumscribe the whole world. That's something which the fastest racehorse could not accomplish."

The sorcerer bowed low: "Since you've unraveled the riddle, I invite you and your royal party to dine with me this evening. Ride straight west through the wood until you come upon my Palace of the Quicken Trees."

Midac's "palace" was actually a pavilion built in the style of the time for entertaining large parties of guests. A circular wooden structure, beautifully carved, pegged, and polished, it had no less than seven doors. At its center, beneath the open smokehole in the roof, a cordial fire blazed. Built-in couches, covered with soft, glossy furs, ringed the fireplace. Finding nobody home, Finn and his men made themselves comfortable. Then their host entered. Midac said not a word. He looked at all of them, turned on his heel, and went out again. At length, Finn spoke.

"My friends, we were invited to a feast. Yet neither food nor drink appears. How strange!"

"Here's something stranger," said Gall Mac Morna. "The fire, which burned clear and fragrant as the flowers of the plain, now fills this hall with a sooty stench and belches up black smoke."

"Here's something stranger than that," said Glas Mac Encarda. "The walls of this place, which were smooth and close-jointed, are now nothing but rough planks, clumsily fastened together with quicken-tree withes."

"Here's something even stranger," said Conan Maol. "The rich rugs and couches have sunk from under us. Here we sit on the bare, damp earth."

"I see something stranger yet," said Foilan. "The seven great doors by which we entered, are gone. A single, narrow, close-fastened exitway is all that remains."

Urgently, Finn spoke again. "You know, my friends, that I never tarry in a house having but one exit. The time has come to leave this foul, smoky den. Get up, one of you, and break down the door."

"That shall be done!" cried Conan. Seizing his spear he planted it on the ground and attempted to spring to his feet—without success. "Alas," he groaned, "this is strangest of all. I find myself firmly fixed to the cold clay floor."

And so it was for each of them.

Beware of easy riddles. Guessing right makes fools of many. Confirmed opinions weigh heavily; they become chains in a way. There's no escape from the enchantment of the "known"—when it's not understood.

At one time or another everyone is made captive. Whether awake or asleep, we can't stir out of the fix in which we find ourselves—caught fast in the Quicken-Tree Palace. King Finn of the Fena, Gall Mac Morna, Glas Mac Encarda, Foilan, and Conan of the frozen spear, move over.

It has happened to me. Once I was invited to speak at a great university. With my head full of the talk I meant to give, I entered the wrong building and found myself in an experimental laboratory where hundreds of caged animals crouched, quivered, barked, screeched, howled, and whined unceasingly, while exuding rank odors of fear, sickness, and pain. I stood among the animals, paralyzed with dismay. They were trying to tell me something. Of that I felt certain. Not just the horror of their condition, but something more.

"Feeling-free science" is science that seeks and exploits knowledge minus understanding, let alone compassion. It profits special interests while undermining the whole world's well-being. Medical research by means of torturing animals to death is only one example. Our dairy, poultry, and red-meat industries feature close-confinement, chemical injections, force-feeding with disgusting materials, hypodermic insemination, and gene manipulation. A U.S. Navy–sponsored project is presently piercing the Pacific from California to Hawaii and beyond with relentlessly repeated underwater voicebox roars of enormous force. Ostensible purpose: to learn how whales and other sea-creatures react. That seems a hardly human response to the songs of the whales.

What has all this got to do with the mythosphere? Plenty. The Hindu epic *Ramayana* and Ovid's *Metamorphoses* both spring to mind. To Indian sensibility, as Ananda Coomeraswami once remarked, "the fundamental feelings, if not the thoughts, of furred and feathered folk are even as our own." And Ovid's masterpiece climaxes in an impassioned plea for fellowship with the animals.

The ancient Greeks and Romans assumed that human slavery was an essential feature of civilization. We assume the same thing about animal abuse. In other words we occupy a quicken-tree palace of our own devising.

The Weighing of the Heart

My late friend J. W. Gould returned from a medical tour of China with some incredible Polaroid shots of open-heart surgery as practiced there. A young woman, not anesthetized, lies smiling serenely up at the camera lens. Acupuncture has rendered her impervious to the shock and pain of the operation. She's alert, wide-eyed as a child, and even seems happy to be photographed. We actually witness this woman's heart laid bare. It's a gaping, gushing crimson valentine between her sallow breasts—all in the same snapshot.

When your head is awake and your heart is laid bare, then where are you? Who or what is looking through your eyes? Who or what is bursting through your heart? Who is smiling?

The Chinese lady in those hospital snaps is actually smiling at us from what constitutes the "being" part of human being. The "being" aspect has nothing to do with nonbeing; it's deathless. And this is what ties every human individual to the human adventure as a whole. Our lives have resonance beyond ourselves. Therefore we can—we should—join hands with mythic blood brothers and blood sisters. Their legends replenish ours, and more than this.

The body has its bloodstream; so does the mind.

* * *

When I suffer physically, the world strikes me as all too physical. When subject to sensuous delight, on the other hand, I appreciate the joyous glory of the physical world. Most of the time, however, events seem only tangentially physical. I can't believe that this is peculiar to me. Surely thoughts, emotions, knowledge, and memory, comprise the bulk of reality is most human lives. That's the portion referred to in ancient Egyptian tomb texts as "the heart." Egyptian myth asserted that the heart may live again, but only if it's feather-light.

As a young child I dreamt that my guardian angel carried me up a ladder and into a great hall where many noble figures sat, with extreme stillness, on thrones built against the walls. I was presented to each of them in turn. Each one leaned forward a little to acknowledge my small and innocently wondering existence. My first visit to Luxor and the Valley of Kings, at age forty-two, reminded me strongly of this dream.

When a Middle-Kingdom Egyptian died and descended to the judgment hall where the feather-goddess Maat presides, what did he find? The tomb texts are explicit. He will have found forty-two judges enthroned, together with Lord Osiris, King of the Dead, ibis-headed Thoth, dog-headed Anubis, falcon-headed Horus, and the goddess of truth herself. And there he will have offered up his heart to be weighed in the balance, against Maat's feather.

If it weigh more than that, a monster devours it.

The pathfinding pathologist William Ober sat in judgment on a daily basis. "Even as weighing the heart was an integral part of Egyptian religion, an essential element in the judgment of the dead," he explained, "so at the autopsy table pathologists of today weigh the heart religiously and form judgments based upon that datum." Here's Ober's sober conclusion:

> From the moral code of the ancient Egyptians through the spiritual values of medieval Christianity, we have arrived at a modern society that prizes quantifiable information as its "summum bonum." . . . Without denying the usefulness of replicable and verifiable empirical data as one of the bases upon which science rests, there is more to science and medicine than coefficients of variance and standard deviation curves. . . . If measurements and numbers can be taken to represent truth, then metaphysics is their feather.

If I read my late friend correctly, he meant that metaphysics is our best remaining substitute for the vanished feather-goddess Maat. Even the most strictly scientific quantifications ought to be weighed in the balance of some larger context. The same goes for moral conduct, artistic creation, and even mythological research.

A fifth-century Coptic papyrus refers to the Archangel Michael as "The Weigher." This document constitutes a bridge between ancient Egyptian and early Christian iconography. The Copts imagined Michael weighing human hearts in the old Egyptian way. Thus Christian funerary practice incorporated something of the Egyptian "Nileboat" tradition. The early Christians also admitted pagan variants whereby the Greek deity Hermes (Latin, "Mercury") took charge of the newly deceased.

When pagan Gaul, Britain, and Ireland were Christianized, the Archangel Michael, or Saint Michael as he came to be known, enfolded their frightened tribes in the shadow of his wings. "On the ruins of ancient temples of Mercury," as Emil Male relates, "rose chapels dedicated to Saint Michael. A hill in La Vendee, even today, bears the significant name of Saint-Michel Mont-Mercure. Saint Michael, already the messenger of heaven, became like Mercury the guide of the dead."

A remarkable fresco by the so-called Michael Master at Vamlingbo church in Gotland represents the soul of a monarch hovering uncertainly in the archangel's balance scales. The cathedral tympanums at Autun and Bourges also show Michael weighing individual souls, represented as miniature nudes, in the balance. So does the one at Paris' Notre Dame Cathedral. A thirteenth-century Catalan altar frontal displays the same scene. Orcagna's fourteenth-century predella at Santa Maria Novella, Florence, introduces an angry devil who tries to tip the scales.

Mont Saint-Michel in Brittany, Mount Saint Michael in Cornwall, and Skellig Michael in Ireland, are actually rocky islets set apart from the shore. All three are places where, in olden times, solemn rites of passage were performed. The dead would then desert "the land of the living" for good. Each one floated afar, aflame, upon a longboat bier.

These thoughts about the distant past bring one's personal future bumpingly to mind. The music stops, and one falls exhausted. Or maybe one develops a charley-horse in swimming and drowns. Something will go wrong, anyhow. Then, death. One's body falls apart, becomes maggots, worms, dust, or fishfood, as the case may be. One's thoughts turn off; those signs on the computer screen wink back into nowhere.

Nowhere! Is there any such place? Not in logic perhaps, but reason says yes. And, according to received scientific opinion, life after death runs directly contrary to the course of nature.

Yet there's another, equally persuasive, position. The common opinion of humankind, as expressed in myth after myth around the globe for generation after generation during many thousands of years, is that something more happens—and will happen. Who are we to dismiss the whole accumulated wisdom of our race?

Regarding any person's life, who can agree? One is just a cough in eternity. Individual consciousness resembles a shoreline strewn with cockleshells, salt-spume, starfish, sandpiper tracks, horse-shoe crabs, seaweed-patterns, sandcastles, and dank tide-maps which the ceaselessly lurching waves erase only to trace anew. If totalities of knowledge exist at all they're well below the blue-blurred horizon. And yet, out by the rocky point, or on that islet in the distance, or else at sea beyond the mists of time, something frightening and wonderful might happen. Who can tell?

Strictly speaking, it's not impossible that we shall undergo some kind of judgment when we die. Painful self-judgment perhaps, with input coming from a wide, fearsome array of divinities, angels, relatives, old friends, and former enemies. And when our hearts have been weighed we may be given further chances to live and grow. To help each other as well.

Or maybe not ever.

> If we understood clearly the difference there
> is between the impossible and the unusual, and
> what is contrary to the course of nature and
> what is contrary to the common opinion of
> mankind, neither believing hastily nor disbe-
> lieving lightly, we should observe the rule,
> "Nothing too much," enjoined by Chilo.

So wrote Michel de Montaigne (1533–1592). Perusing his pages, as Ralph Waldo Emerson remarked, "is like touching a living man." I especially admire this confessional philosopher, whose name so weirdly mirrors Mont Saint-Michel. He fought in a foul religious war without losing either his head or his chivalry. His *Essais* were totally unprecedented plunges into subjective research. He referred to the secrets of his own being as "my physics and my metaphysics." He was skeptical and yet faithful at the same time. Our modern, dubious, and self-consciously juggling cast of mind commenced with him.

Morally, however, we've come no distance since Montaigne's day. We still resemble secret societies on legs. Or else we're like a sinister visitor whom I once encountered hovering in the brilliant shallows off a Bahamian sandbar—my own shadow.

Montaigne internalized the Archangel Michael. He weighed his own heart as well as he could. That was heroic. It pointed ahead to an unfulfilled human goal.

Backhoe at Olympia

Fully fifty percent of the Greek people were routinely disadvantaged in pagan times, because female. Moreover, up to twenty percent were slaves. The remaining population of free males were notably quarrelsome and uncharitable. That's the dark side of classical culture. Yet Greek myth, art, literature, ritual, drama, and especially sport, all indicate a prevailingly healthy attitude. By and large the classical Greeks stood up to life in cheerful, self-disciplined, well-measured style. They portrayed their divinities as glorious and above all happy beings. They themselves strove to resemble gods, especially on the athletic fields at Olympia. Hard, happy play especially delighted them.

The first Olympic Games occurred way back in 776 B.C. The classical era dates from that event. It came to an end no less than 1,169 years later, when the last games were held in A.D. 393. During its heyday, Olympia was a tight complex of athletic fields, tracks, viewing stands, public buildings, shrines, colonnaded temples, and many thousands of statues. The most admired monument was Phidias' huge, long-vanished "chryselephantine" (gold and ivory) statue of Zeus. Majestically seated in its own immense temple, this was counted among the Seven Wonders of the ancient world. A few connoisseurs complained that if the Zeus of Phidias were to arise from his throne he would break through the temple roof, but why not?

"God is great."

The Byzantine Emperor Theodosius abolished the Games and toppled Olympia's temples. Then came floods, earthquakes, and the tidal attrition of time itself. Present-day Olympia has no pomp and no splendor. Instead it's got wildflowers, trees, history, and tumbled stones. The drums of some columns remain more or less as they fell, in freeze-frame, as it were.

When visiting Olympia I used to spend some daytime hours at the Archeological Museum, but most of them outdoors. I raced with my children in the stadium, argued with their mother on the foundations of the "House of Phidias," reread the classic texts while slouched on a shady bench, or wandered off to daydream with my back against a column of Hera's temple. The moist soft breeze, the shiplike clouds, the broken conchiferate columns crisp with fossilized seashells, the nightingales, the poppies, and the asphodels, all combined to induce a kind of time travel for me. They helped my thoughts unscroll upon the dappled silvery light.

The pagan deities were never team players; hence, no team play occurred at ancient Olympia. Individual excellence was all that mattered there. Zeus was believed to have wrestled his father Cronus in the first Olympic Games, thus wrenching the kingdom of heaven from the old man's iron grasp. The sun god Apollo, who raced across the known world every day, was said to have outsprinted Hermes, guide of souls. Apollo also outboxed Ares, the battle deity, with sunstroke jabs.

Historically, the cattle-rich city-state of Elis, which included Olympia within her territory, sponsored the Games. Every four years she would send out "truce-bearers of Zeus the thunder god" to issue invitations among a hundred or more widely scattered Greek cities, from Marseilles in the west to Trebizond on the Black Sea. A one-month "truce of Greece" was proclaimed for the occasion. Any Hellenic power that molested travelers or made war during the sacred time was subject to strict penalties. About a thousand athletes and their trainers would be welcomed at Olympia, along with some 45,000 spectators.

Part sport, part religion, and part World's Fair, the Games took place over a five-day period during the first full moon of August or September. Menander encapsulated the fringe life of the Olympic Festival as: "Crowd, market, entertainers, acrobats, thieves." The first day of the ancient Olympics was reserved for greetings, meetings, and oath-takings, plus a special sacrifice to "Zeus, Averter of Flies." No one can say precisely what that sacrifice was or how it worked. However, Aelian assures us that all resident flies buzzed off, "purely out of respect for the god."

The Games made it possible for good men to value their neighbors (including distant neighbors) as individual opponents, and to compete with them according to strict rules of play. Only a god can worship a god in the fullest way. Only a champion athlete can compete at top form with a fellow champion. And though they come from the ends of the earth, they'll understand one another.

The fifth and final day of the Games was given over to festivities culminating in a great open-air banquet at which victory odes were sung. Pindar composed the most famous of all such odes, which begins:

> Single is the race, single,
> of men and gods.
> From a single mother we both
> draw breath.

On my last visit to Olympia I found a horde of part-time laborers swarming over the grounds. Some were busily backhoeing a trench deep into the Hill of Cronus, which overlooks the sacred precinct. Others were using power saws to sweep away the gigantic old pine trees that lent such solemn grandeur to the scene. Meanwhile the majority sat around assiduously plucking weeds and picking at lichen plus whatever bits of soil had settled, century by century, in tiny chinks, cracks and pockmarks of the temple stones.

Upon making inquiries, I was referred to the foreman, who in turn referred me to the Director of the Archeological Museum. So I went there and phoned the Director from the front desk. While declining to meet with me or to discuss my complaint, she did at least hear me out.

I then sought solace from the museum's incomparable collection of archaic and classical bronzes, but there again I got a shock. Gone was the verdigris, the green patina that centuries-long exposure imparts to bronze surfaces. All sense of life and breath had vanished as well, from every single statuette. The whole lot stood chemically bathed and polished down, reduced to dolly-deities and chocolate soldiery. Timeless things especially require the caress of time. When that's withdrawn they seize up. Rigor mortis sets in. I was reminded of a hermetic text called "Rosarium Philosophorum," published in Basel in 1593:

> Thou hast inquired about the greenness, deeming the bronze to be a leprous body on account of the greenness it hath upon it. Therefore I say unto thee that whatever is perfect in the bronze is that greenness only!

Feeling like a one-eyed person in the kingdom of the blind, I passed the night between bad dreams and gloomy thoughts. Modern education, plus the commercial attrition of contemporary life, produce a cauterizing effect. The skin of one's psyche turns glassy, scarred, and shut. "For man has closed himself up," as William Blake lamented, "till he sees all things through the narrow chinks of his cavern."

Next morning, on the Hill of Cronus, I observed a lady ordering the laborers to cease work. They didn't want to do it; not because they loved the labor but because the pay was good. As natives of Olympia's tourist-oriented village, they felt that they deserved a piece of the action. So a shouting match ensued, and the backhoe operator angrily reversed his machine into the remains of a temple wall, damaging both.

I had to laugh.

The pagan Greeks believed that their ancestors were the same as their gods' ancestors. Both mortals and immortals sprang from Gaia, Mother Earth. Therefore the Greeks stood tall, in cousinly relation to the divine. From our shamefaced, guilt-ridden perspective, classical Greece may seem to have been a place of vainglorious and somewhat crazy behavior. But we are the unhealthy ones, not they. Like the bronze statuary at Olympia's Archeological Museum, we also have passed through an acid bath. As human-kind's capacities have grown, our confidence has diminished.

Why?

Pagan poets such as Homer, Pindar, and Ovid plainly felt comfortable with their gods' eternal youth. Generally speaking, our own deities are neither youthful nor fun to contemplate. They assume relatively didactic, not to say punishing, roles in our lives. Worst of all, contemporary deities are themselves unhappy!

In modern Christianity, Islam, Judaism, Buddhism, and Hinduism, where's the sense of play?

Raging Dove

Beyond the salt borders of Eire, Colum Cille is known as Saint Columba—Latin for "dove." The most terrible-tempered saint in history, he was born a Druid Prince in a converted Catholic family. His story demonstrates the fact that righteous anger is not necessarily negative. One need not be a wimp in order to be good. And to actually do good, which is far more important, a degree of passion is actually required.

By way of inculcating an appetite for letters, Columba's mother nourished the child on alphabet cakes. At seven he began his studies with the castle priest. Nine years later, at sixteen, Columba was ordained. He then took to the roads, traveling the length and breadth of Ireland in search of enlightenment. The saint's biography, composed by a disciple shortly after his death, contains the following anecdote:

> He reached the dwelling-place of Longarad Whitefoot, a master in theology, history, law, and poetry. Colum Cille came to be his guest, but Lon hid his books from him. So Colum left a curse on the books. "May that which you have begrudged me be useless after you!"

he said. And so it was. For the books are still amongst us, yet no man can read them.

Longarad's books were probably composed in the ancient Ogham script, which was already becoming indecipherable. Either that, or else the esoteric master employed some cryptographic snarl of his own devising. In either case, he evidently feared that Columba's piercing eye might penetrate to things that were better left dark.

At age forty, Columba prepared to settle down at Moville Abbey, under the tutelage of its Abbot: learned Saint Finnian. The Abbot had accomplished an arduous, indeed almost impossible, pilgrimage. He'd gone all the way to Rome and returned with a priceless treasure: Saint Jerome's Latin translation of the New Testament. It was the only copy in all Ireland. As a token of trusting affection, Saint Finnian loaned this book to Columba for a week.

Secretly intent upon copying Jerome's version for himself, Colum Cille holed up in his cell. Not for nothing was he known as "Columba of the Quick Hand." The work went so well that by the end of the seventh day it neared completion.

Columba kept a pet crane with him in his cell; isn't that a curious detail? Looking out through the large keyhole on that final afternoon, the crane observed an eye pressed to the outer side. Instantly, as if to spear a fish, Columba's guardian struck with her beak through the keyhole. A fellow monk had crouched outside the door to spy. Now he ran off down the corridor "with his eye lying along his cheek." Screaming, he staggered into the Abbot's quarters. Saint Finnian deftly restored the meddling monk's eyeball to its socket. That done, he padded along to Columba's cell.

Flinging open the door, Finnian shouted: "Give back my book, and your copy, too!"

Columba handed over the original, but refused to part with his copy. "The word of God belongs to all," he explained. On matters of literature, even saints differ, and now the first copyright wrangle in recorded history got underway. The case was appealed through the courts until at last it came before the High King at Tara, who handed down this verdict:

"To every cow her calf, and to every book its transcript. The copy that Columba made belongs to Finnian!"

With that, Columba's priestly vows went glimmering. His warrior heritage manifested itself. "This is a wrong decision!" he declared. Turning, brimful of fury, he strode out from the High King's hall. Riding home to Donegal, he raised a rebel force amongst his kinsmen. At its head, he boldly marched back east into Meath, where he challenged the King to battle. Their forces met on the field of Culdreihmne. By nightfall, three thousand warriors lay dead. The King had fled, but Colum Cille gained nothing. Public opinion turned against him.

Convoking a synod at Teltown, the Irish bishops laid a penance upon their headstrong cleric. For each of the three thousand slain in the "Battle of the Book," the bishops proclaimed, Columba must convert a heathen soul to Christ. Unpredictable as ever, Colum Cille bowed to this order. He resolved to spread the Gospel in "Albion of the Ravens," as Scotland was called.

The saint prepared a coracle, a sailing dinghy made of cowhides stretched over a willow frame. Twelve disciples sailed with him. A brisk south wind favored their voyage northeastward. The sea sparkled; Columba wept and sang. On May the thirteenth, in A.D. 563, their little boat nosed in amongst the felspar and olivenite pebbles of a small island shore. They had reached Iona, off Mull, in the western Hebrides. Climbing the small green hill which overlooked the cove, Columba searched the horizon. No smudge of home was to be seen.

Satisfied, he blessed the hill on which he stood, naming it "Cairn Cul-ri-Erin," or "Cairn of the Arse to Ireland."

Having established his little colony on Iona, Columba journeyed to the mainland to pay court to the pagan Pict who ruled the whole region. But dark King Brude's Druid advisors barred the castle gates against Columba. Hopping mad, the saint called upon the powers of heaven for help. Thereupon a rosy-winged angel loomed up at his back— assisting Columba to sail right over the gate.

King Brude confessed to being impressed. He quickly confirmed the still seething saint's possession of Iona. He also granted permission for the founding of no less than three hundred and sixty-five churches along the Scottish and Northumbrian coasts. In good time, that was done. Columba converted, not three thousand, but some three hundred thousand Picts, with King Brude at their head.

One day, while the saint was sitting amongst his disciples in the oratory at Iona, the book satchels

which lined the shelves along the walls all crashed
down together in dusty thunder. Their sheepskin
bindings split apart. The parchment codices splayed
out across the floor. Stunned silence followed.
Then, after a long moment for reflection, Columba spoke.

"Longarad, master of every art, is dead in
Ossary!"

The monk who was destined to write the saint's
biography rolled his eyes in horror. "Let's hope
you're mistaken!" he exclaimed.

"For that I put a curse on you," Columba fumed.
"May your word always be doubted, too!" And so
it was.

Letters soon arrived from Ireland confirming that
the old sorcerer had expired at the very hour when
the book satchels fell. Longarad's departing spirit
had brushed roughly by Iona. But why?

Longarad, remember, had carefully concealed his
own books from Colum Cille's gaze. Making a
mystery of literature, he suffered in consequence.
Lon's lonely lifetime's delving in the esoteric realm
came to naught. His library was illegible, and nothing could be done to remove Columba's curse upon
it. But there might still be time to inspire fresh li-
braries. So at the final moment of his life the old
occultist bethought himself to signal an ancient en-
emy. With his last breath, the "master of every art"
lurched forth over Iona.

There, as codice after broken codice loudly tumbled down across the flagstone floor, Longarad
stopped to seize the prickly saint by the hair and
hiss imperatively in Columba's ear. With no word
spoken, the longtime enmity between the two men

was transformed into a bond stronger than death. Together, they achieved a very positive result.

"Columba of the Quick Hand" turned his energies from proselytizing to publishing. The saint set up a scriptorium. Under Colum Cille's direction, the monastery at Iona produced hundreds of illuminated Gospels and psalters.

Classical aesthetics calls for clean-lined subordination of parts to the whole, but Celtic style is just the opposite. The books produced at Iona had high initial letters writhing in rainbow play, flaunting their tails hither and yon, twining about, nuzzling and even biting each other, upon page after page of ivory-toned vellum. Sunbursts of bright yellow orpiment, dragons with red lead wings, forests in deep green acetate of copper, sapphire skies and lamp-black caverns were to be discovered there.

Distributed as far afield as Italy and Spain, Iona's elaborately glowing manuscripts inspired thousands of European monks to creative emulation. Like messenger birds with iridescent necks, sacred manuscripts flocked forth for the illumination of Europe.

Tear-Away Treasure

Cultural evolution proceeds indirectly by means of ongoing processes such as creation, translation, interpretation, trial, error, and displacement. In dreams also, as Sigmund Freud observed, displacement plays a crucial role. Among actual displacements, the most acute come about through conquest.

Consider what the Frankish crusaders and their Venetian allies wrought in 1204, when they turned upon the very city that was hosting their campaign. Byzantine Constantinople was by far the wealthiest, most beautiful place that the beer-swilling, illiterate Franks had ever seen. Its citizens were educated, haughty, and refined. The soldiers of Christ could not resist the temptation to put the silk-clad Constantinopolitans down and rob them blind during three days and nights of full-out pillage and slaughter. That was the single most suicidal act in the entire history of Christendom.

It so happened that the city's five hundred Orthodox Christian churches, together with their cloisters and nunneries, all possessed sacred relics of a historic or mortuary nature, sumptuously encased in jewel-encrusted gold or silver reliquaries.

During the pillage the clergy were slaughtered at their altars, the nuns were raped, and the relics removed.

Venetian connoisseurs made off with four mettlesome chariot horses of gilded bronze, dating from classical times. This radiantly lovely chariot team had been spirited away from ancient Olympia in order to amuse an early Byzantine emperor. Now it was piously installed on the exterior balcony over the main doors of San Marco Basilica at Venice.

Plundered in the same sack were the Head of Saint James, the Body of Saint Andrew, the Head of Saint John Chrysostom, a splinter of the True Cross, the Crown of Thorns, the Forefinger of Doubting Thomas, the Head of Saint Stephen Protomartyr, and not one but two Heads of John the Baptist. These items now repose in churches at Halberstadt, Amalfi, Pisa, Bromholm, Sens, Soissons, and Amiens, respectively.

"God works in mysterious ways"—not excluding forcible displacements from one culture to another. It could be argued that the sudden shift of Byzantine religious relics to Western Europe revitalized many a rustic bishopric, while confirming the pastoral power of the Roman Catholic Church. Around each relic, meanwhile, stories grew. Thus they contributed to legend, as well.

The wild Western races' fading memories of pagan gods were replaced by "Lives of the Saints."

So much for the westward displacement of Christian culture in crusader times. During the nineteenth century a second westward displacement occurred. This was begun by Thomas Bruce, the seventh Earl of Elgin. He loved Hellenic antiquities, yet felt no particular affection for Greece herself. In those days Athens was just a dusty and forlorn provincial capital, under the Turkish slipper. What Lord Elgin most wanted in life was to loot the marble sculptures from her ancient Acropolis. As British ambassador to Istanbul, Elgin brought diplomatic pressure to bear upon the Sublime Porte, and obtained the needed permissions.

In twelve months his three hundred Athenian workmen stripped from the Parthenon seventeen large sculptures of pagan immortals, fifteen low-relief metopes, and a long frieze which shows men, women, horses, and sacrificial animals in procession. For good measure they threw in a "caryatid" (a column in the form of a maiden) from the portico of a neighboring temple: the Erechtheum. All together, Elgin's crew filled two hundred crates with marble carvings for transport home on a British warship.

> Noseless himself, he brings home noseless blocks,
> To show at once the ravages of time and pox.

So Elgin's fellow peer, Lord Byron, spitefully remarked. Next, government officials tweaked the proud Scot's button-nose. Citing "abuse of privilege" in the matter of the warship, they soon diddled the crestfallen collector out of his incredibly splendid haul. Objective: to enrich the British Museum.

That's where the "Elgin Marbles" reside today. Everyone who can possibly do so should go and see them at least once or twice. Take time to contemplate each carving. It will gleam in rhythm with your own breath. It will even seem to move, flowing with utmost grace and even exuberance, against the grain of your gaze.

When Actress Melina Mercouri was appointed Athens' Minister of Culture, she raised a rich, melodious cry for the return of the Elgin Marbles to Greece. British authorities snickered, coughed, shuffled their feet, and turned their profiles.

For piratical audacity, the British antiquarian Charles Cockerell stood second only to Elgin himself. Cockerell stripped his loot from Aphaia's temple on the island of Aegina. The extraordinarily well-preserved carvings that he carried off had been created near the start of the fifth century B.C. In 1812, King Ludwig of Bavaria obtained them at auction. Now residing at Munich's Archeological Museum, the Aegina marbles rival Elgin's in importance. Munich's "Crouching Hercules," for example, presents a shatteringly clear ideal of heroic calm.

As Cockerell prepared to slip away from Greece, a friendly Turkish official suggested with a wink that he might do well to wheel a cart past the base of the Acropolis on departure night. "I accordingly arranged this," Cockerell wrote. "As I drew near the Acropolis there was a shout from above to look out, and without further warning the block which formed one of the few remaining pieces of the southern frieze of the Parthenon was bowled down the cliff. My men successfully caught it and put in the cart."

In 1871 a German railway engineer named Carl Humann wrote to a friend ecstatically from Turkish

Pergamon: "Remember the high thick wall in which I showed you the two sculptures projecting from underneath? I have now got these out and at home, on Prussian ground!" Humann eventually made off with the whole Hellenistic altar of Pergamon, with its stormily histrionic 400-foot frieze, for rebuilding in Berlin.

All told, sublime classical sculpture by the hundreds of tons tumbled into western Europe during the nineteenth century. And this truly massive displacement was multiplied in effect by the production of plaster casts taken from the originals. Soon such casts stood in every art school and provincial museum, across Europe and also in America.

That helped shape Victorian culture. The British and Germans in particular became drunk on Spartan warrior ideals and Alexandrian visions of empire. Thus both sides were seduced into the nightmare mudslide of World War One.

As hundreds of tales and films concerning the "Mummy's Curse" or variations thereof attest, the strangest and least well-assimilated cultural displacement in modern times was from ancient Egypt. In an 1881 bulletin of the Egyptian Institute, archeologist Gaston Maspero excitedly described unearthing dozens of pharaohs' mummies from a cavern in the Valley of Kings:

> Three days later the Museum's steamer arrived and no sooner was it loaded than it set sail back to Bulaq with its cargo of kings. A strange thing happened! From Luxor to Quft on both banks of the Nile the wailing fellahin

women with disheveled hair followed the
boat, and the men fired off their guns, just as
they do at funerals.

Shortly before his assassination, the deeply civilized Egyptian President Anwar Sadat made a general request. Every nation in possession of an
ancient Egyptian mummy, he pleaded, should give
it back to Egypt for reverent reinterment. This idea
was greeted with innocent merriment worldwide.

The antiquities in anyone's collection or local
museum are apt to have been forcibly seized, de-
viously acquired, or stolen outright at least once,
and generally smuggled from one place to another.
That's the shadow-side of the art world. Most great
museums possess extensive holdings in tribal, ritual, and mortuary art objects, plus religious works
that have been ripped from sacred places around
the globe.

Science is brilliantly equipped to measure and
weigh antiquities and to plumb archeological remains, but the religious impulses of the human psyche cannot be measured, weighed, or plumbed.
Besides, all art worthy of the name is spiritual in
its degree. And who are we to despise the pious
instincts of any people on earth? We've been taught
to look upon museums as modern temples of culture. So they are, but what kind of culture do they
actually represent?

Our postmodern mindset is broadly eclectic, fe-
verishly acquisitive, doggedly curious—and cold
unto death.

The Denver Museum holds no less than fifteen
thousand Native American objects, mostly of un-

certain provenance. Among these, until recently, was an austere Zuni woodcarving of a war god. When Zuni tribal elders demanded its return, an air-conditioned powwow ensued. From one viewpoint the object in question symbolized an archetype which exists in everyone's "collective unconscious." To keep such a thing on public display for discussion and analysis was therefore educational, right, and good. But what if the object were in fact a sacred mystery? What if the people who thought they "got it," didn't?

The Zunis claimed to have a historic mutual understanding of the object. They alone felt qualified to interact with it in a religious context. And so, after weeks of deliberation the carving was regretfully relinquished to the Zuni people, who returned it to a secret home in the desert.

Future discussions, reevaluations, and redistributions are called for. Not just at Denver, either. We should go beyond curiosity and begin to show concern for the mythic heritage of every race. As the Earth shrinks and people multiply, displacement no longer works in any positive sense.

Cherishment emerges.

Ancestral Voices

When I close my eyes at night, preparing for sleep, the darkness in back of my eyelids sparkles with phosphors. This tells me that light shines everywhere, whether the darkness knows it or not. Tonight, I'm wondering about my maternal Irish ancestors.

Some years ago a Limerick boy went digging for potatoes within the walls of an ancient fortified farm called Ardagh, south of the river Shannon. He felt his spade strike something firmer and more smooth than any spud. The point of his spade turned the object up out of the earth. It winked and gleamed like a live thing. Wondering, the boy reached in amongst the thornbush roots to wrench his find from the black loam. The sun shone once again upon the most wondrous metalwork in Ireland.

For permanence, mold lowly clay, or carve a stone. Whatever is made of precious metals cries out to be stolen, broken up, or melted down. The "Ardagh Chalice," as it has come to be known, is of gold and silver, yet strangely this dates from at least as far back as the eighth century of our era. That is, from the dark days when Viking invaders poleaxed Ireland. Did some doomed Christian abbot secretly inter the chalice in order to preserve it from Danish drinking bouts?

Was it recovered, only to go underground again when Normans in chain mail, Elizabethans in velvet, and Puritans in broadcloth arrived to harrow the Queen of Ireland's soul? Kathleen Ni Houlihan revives, returns, forever virgin, and this chalice belongs to her. It's only seven inches high and yet so heavy that a strong man must use both hands to drink from it. The hollow silver bulge of the chalice creates a generous reflection of the showery Irish sky. Its beaded gold ornamentation imitates the yellow sea-wrack riding in and out upon the tidewaters of Eire. Its stained glass studs, inset with veinlike bronze, are like warm tears.

The base of the grail is a hollow hemisphere which conceals a luminous crystal set in gold. Raise up the cup, tilt it as if to drink the wine of Holy Communion, and the crystal brilliantly manifests.

A while ago I was in the train, and getting near Sligo. . . . A man got into the carriage and began to play on a fiddle made apparently of an old blacking-box, and though I am quite unmusical the sounds filled me with the strangest emotions. I seemed to hear a voice of lamentation out of the Golden Age. It told me that we are imperfect, incomplete, and no more like a beautiful woven web, but like a bundle of cords knotted together and flung into a corner. . . . It said that if only they who live in the Golden Age could die we might be happy, for the sad voices would be still; but

202 · *The Timeless Myths*

they must sing and we must weep until the
eternal gates swing open.

There's a silver breath of sweetness to that mystical account. It's from *The Celtic Twilight* (1893) by
William Butler Yeats.

"Love thy neighbor!" comes a cry from the pulpit.
"Kill for your country!" says the state, and one
hardly knows what to think. "Carry on hating forever!" So most racial, religious, and class traditions
insist, even today, in their insidiously whispering
way. Such injunctions tend to cancel each other out.
Moralities of love and hate which are rooted in obe-
dience to the commands of custom, church, and
state, will topple when the wind is high.

The individual way of strength and flexibility is
to value one's enemies, thanking and honoring each
one for the challenges they bring. We should practice forbearance to all enemies—both within and
without. Measured forbearance holds steady even
in combat. But combat "to the death" defeats itself.

To destroy one's enemies is like biting off one's
own fingers.

The Gaelic "Yellow Book of Lecan" at Trinity
College, Dublin, contains a stirring account of a
voyage made about the year A.D. 700 by the Irish
hero Maildun. Most of this narrative is mythic, yet
hung from a historic frame. It provides a kind of
answer to the angry sea-roar which surrounds the
island coast of every human heart.

Maildun's mission was to locate the freebooting
seamen who had raided his homeland. He sought
vengeance for his father, Allil Ocar Aga, cut down

at the church of Dooclone. With sixty-two comrades, Maildun sailed for a day, a night, and another day, out across the open sea. On the second evening the adventurers reached an island. A fine mansion stood at the water's edge. From it came a tumult of rough voices, singing, merry shouts, and then this:

"Stand off from me, for I'm the best warrior here! I'm the man who killed Allil Ocar Aga and burned Dooclone over his head! No man has dared avenge Allil, nor ever will."

Hearing those words, Maildun's heart leapt for joy. "Now, surely," said his comrades, "Heaven has guided our ship to this place! Here is an easy victory. Let us now sack this house, since God has revealed our enemies to us, and delivered them into our hands!" But while they were speaking the wind arose and a great tempest broke suddenly upon them. And they were driven violently before the storm, all night and part of the next day, over the boundless ocean.

"Lower the sail," Maildun commanded at last. "Draw your oars inboard. Now let us drift before the wind like children, wherever God wishes us to go."

Trials and perils lay ahead. Maildun and his men visited the isle of monstrous ants, the terraced isle of birds, the palace of solitude, the isle of red-hot animals, the isle of weeping, the palace of the little cat, the black-and-white isle, the palace of the crystal spring, the isle of the burning river, the isle of the four precious walls, the big blacksmiths' isle, the silver pillar of the sea, the isle of the mystic lake, and finally the isle of laughing. After many years, the ship circled back to the island of Maildun's enemies, and the mansion that he had been about to sack. Now he and his men crept up to the great front door. The people inside were at dinner, and this was their conversation:

"As to Maildun," said the first, "it's well known that he drowned long ago in the great ocean."

"Don't be too sure," said the second. "Maildun may show up someday to give us a rude awakening."

"If he were to come," said the third, "what should we do?"

"That's easy," said the fourth—and Maildun smiled, for he recognized the voice. "Maildun has suffered great hardships for a long time. We were enemies once, it's true. However, if he were to arrive here this minute I'd offer a glad welcome!"

Loudly knocking, Maildun announced himself. He and his men were soon inside, joyfully received on every hand. Hot baths and fresh garments were given them. Feasting and merriment followed. And the following night, having rested well, Maildun told of all the wonders that God had revealed to him and his men upon the broad, mysterious ocean.

According to Celtic legend, the Tuatha de Danann, or people of the goddess Danu, preceded the Celts themselves in Ireland. "Brugh na Boyne" was the best of their fairy palaces. Their chief, or "Dagda," kept the Boyne residence for himself while distributing the other palaces among his sons—all except for Angus, the youngest.

Angus protested. "At least," he said, "lend me Brugh na Boyne to occupy alone for a day and a night."

"Fair enough!" said the Dagda.

After twenty-four hours had passed the king went to reclaim his property, but Angus refused to leave.

"You never said that any particular day and night were meant," the youth explained. "This palace belongs to me until day and night shall cease to be!"

"What?" cried the Dagda in shock. But then on second thought, with a proud paternal smile, he acquiesced.

Carbon-dating indicates that the monumental mausoleum at New Grange, Ireland, was built in truly ancient times, before the Great Pyramids of Egypt arose. Now, the traditional name for New Grange is Brugh na Boyne.

It contains 250,000 tons of material, or about five million manloads. It is three hundred feet in diameter and seventy feet high. The single small square doorway gives access to a sixty-foot passage which expands inward to a chamber with a lofty "beehive" dome. Huge, slab-sided boulders, cantilevered inward, line the dark interior. This whole incredibly massive structure was designed with extreme mathematical precision and engineered accordingly. New Grange was oriented to sunrise at the time of the winter solstice. Ireland is rainy, but it's fairly safe to say that on at least one morning between the nineteenth and the twenty-third of December the rays of the rising sun would pass through a slit in the roof to illuminate the tomb chamber.

Since we know nothing about them, it's tempting to assume that the "New Grange people," as archeologists call the Tuatha de Danann, were less intelligent than ourselves. They are pictured as hairy, hunched and unwashed prey to primitive superstition. But there's no evidence to support such assumptions.

Superstition has been defined as credulous belief in things that don't exist. But there's also negative superstition, meaning disbelief in things that do exist. Either way, it's safe to say that everyone, in every generation, is prone to ignorance and error regarding such matters. If archeologists were to excavate a modern cyclotron five thousand years hence, what might they make of it? Superstition, probably.

Looking up from the hollow eye-sockets of their skulls, the dead at New Grange will have "seen" successions of cloud-spirals carved into the megalithic dome. What for? What was the point of all this brilliant artfulness and hard human labor? There is no answer. In fact, it's by no means certain that New Grange was built as a burial site. My own guess is that this became a tomb after its original purpose had been forgotten.

Imagine a pre–Celtic ritual ordeal, one which the later Druids adopted and modified for their own open-air practice. This concerns coming-of-age: A prince of the Tuatha de Danann is to be initiated. He must undergo a midwinter vigil. It's a lost traveler's dream under Brugh na Boyne, the seventy-foot hill. Interred in the interior chamber with its cloud-patterned dome, the youth lies all alone. Shivering in the silence, with a quarter-million tons of earth and stone bearing down upon him, he experiences a long-drawn sort of death.

Then finally the solstice sunbeams appear. They come curving down the inside of his cold, dark place of fear. At this point the youth remembers his relation to the goddess Danu. Among her other names is Cessair, the mother of Circe. The youth has ceased to tremble. Those golden rays illuminate his true philosophical inheritance. He gains a deep, firm sense of day and night. Home, that is: the living embrace of time. Not until he was made aware of this could Angus come into his own as a Knight of the Round Table.

Many are the saints, painters, and poets, both male and female, who belong to the same timeless fellowship. It's ours to join as well. You may ask, precisely what Round Table do I mean? The one that's come to be associated with the Druid sorcerer Merlin and King Arthur? Yes, certainly, but there is more. The Round Table is what's "given," God knows why or how, and accepted in a heartfelt way. It's the reality that you and I have sat talking about for the past hour.

Hubris, anger, and ignorance beset us from inside. We make mistakes, and worse. Yet thanks to the swirling mythosphere, our adventure is timeless. And everywhere four saving thrusts recur:

Light shines in darkness.
Frontiers open to fresh vistas.
Love follows hard upon enmity.
From what is hidden comes revelation.

All myth tends to conclude in one or more of these four saving thrusts, which carry the considerable freight of challenge and consolation alike. Art, at its best, does the same. Light shines in the darkness of Edward Hopper's *Nighthawks*, for example, and it irradiates the Sunflower Maiden who came in from the dew to share a Kansas farmer's iron cot. Every sunrise and sunset shows frontiers opening to fresh vistas. They opened for the Han Emperor's daughter when she sent her spirit-body to consort with General Wu, and for me when I dreamed of Mount Fuji. In the case of Circe and Odysseus, love followed hard upon enmity. Saint Columbia laid an irreversible curse upon Longarad's books, yet at the moment of his death the Magus lovingly shook the Saint into book publishing. In Pieter Brueghel's *Massacre of the Innocents*, revelation springs from what is hidden. It zigzags from the seemingly unpaintable out there to the seemingly unknowable within oneself. Michel de Montaigne weighed his own hidden heart, thus internalizing the Archangel Michael. That's something which we too can try and do.

Index

DUTTON Ⓟ **PLUME** (0452)

SCIENTIFIC THOUGHT

☐ **COSMIC VOYAGE** *A Scientific Discovery of Extraterrestrials Visiting Earth* by **Courtney Brown, Ph.D.** Based on unprecedented proof, this work breaks new ground in the search for extraterrestrial life. Shocking, revealing, moving, and ultimately inspiring, it not only reveals vital new data about alien visitors, but provides insights into our own spiritual existence and even offers the first demonstrable proof of the existence of the human soul. "Takes us on an extraordinary journey into some of the deepest mysteries of alien contact and the human future . . . A wonderful, audacious and important book."—Whitley Strieber (940987—$23.95)

☐ **FRONTIERS II** *More Recent Discoveries about Life, Earth, Space, and the Universe* by **Isaac and Janet Asimov.** This gathering of 125 of Asimov's last, best science essays spans the full spectrum of new scientific knowledge, taking us onto the brink of tomorrow. There is no more infectiously enthusiastic guide to science than the incomparable Isaac Asimov and his wonder-filled and illuminating book. "Far-ranging and entertaining."—*Library Journal* (272297—$12.95)

☐ **WE ARE NOT ALONE** *The Continuing Search for Extraterrestrial Intelligence. Revised Edition.* by **Walter Sullivan.** In this completely updated version of his bestselling classic, the renowned science correspondent for the *New York Times* examines past breakthroughs and recent discoveries, as well as the latest technological advances to objectively sum up strong evidence for the existence of alien civilizations and shows how we might find and communicate with them. "A fascinating book"—*New York Times Book Review* (272246—$13.95)

Prices slightly higher in Canada.

Visa and Mastercard holders can order Plume, Meridian, and Dutton books by calling
1-800-253-6476.
They are also available at your local bookstore. Allow 4-6 weeks for delivery.
This offer is subject to change without notice.

MD12

Ⓟ **PLUME**

WORLD ISSUES

☐ **DON'T BELIEVE THE HYPE** *Fighting Cultural Misinformation about African-Americans* **by Farai Chideya.** This book is filled with factual ammunition for fighting the stereotypes and misinformation too often accepted as the "truth" about the 31 million African-Americans in this country. The author draws on hard fact, not hype to show the real picture on key subjects like jobs, education, social welfare, crime, politics, and affirmative action. (270960—$11.95)

☐ **WHICH SIDE ARE YOU ON?** *Trying to Be for Labor When It's Flat on Its Back* **by Thomas Geoghegan.** This gripping epic of economic loss and shattered dreams demands we take a fresh look at the dilemmas of class in modern America, and at ourselves. "Brilliant, inspiring . . . charming and acidic at once . . . unparalleled in the literature of American labor."—*New York Times Book Review* (268915—$12.95)

☐ **THE LITIGATION EXPLOSION** *What Happened When America Unleashed the Lawsuit* **by Walter K. Olson.** From malpractice suits to libel actions, from job discrimination to divorce, suing first and asking questions later has become a way of life in the United States. Here is the first major exploration of this trend—why it developed, who profits and who loses, and how it can be contained. (268249—$13.95)

☐ **THE AGE OF MISSING INFORMATION by Bill McKibben.** In this brilliant, provocative exploration of ecology and the media, McKibben demolishes our complacent notion that we are "better informed" than any previous generation. "By turns humorous, wise, and troubling . . . a penetrating critique of technological society."—*Cleveland Plain Dealer* (269806—$11.95)

Prices slightly higher in Canada.

Visa and Mastercard holders can order Plume, Meridian, and Dutton books by calling **1-800-253-6476.**
They are also available at your local bookstore. Allow 4-6 weeks for delivery.
This offer is subject to change without notice.

PL44